KIM BRIGHT

Someone Borrowed, Someone Blue

*To Rebeccah,
Thank you.
Healing Happens!*

SM

Contents

II   The Invitation to Heal

III   Start Right Here

IV   Forgiveness is a Dirty Job

V   Masks Won't Hide You From Your Secrets

VI   The Womb Was Created to Create

VII The Finish Line

VIII Begin Again

IX Drafts Folder

Dedication

In loving memory of Jamilah
(Donita Jones)

You were right. Healing happens.

Acknowledgments

As many times as I have stopped and started this book over the course of 13 years, I know that it would've never seen the light of day without the consistent and extraordinary support of some extraordinary people:

First. Thank you, God, for being the Restorer of my soul, and for allowing me to be a living, breathing testimony of your faithfulness and power to heal... *like it never happened.*

To my husband, Art, you've had a front-row, back row, *and* backstage view of my healing and book journey. I love you and appreciate every cheer, hug, neck rub, plate of food (because you knew I wasn't going to take a break), and holding down our world, especially during the final stretch. Everything I know about music production, I learned it from you — and now I have a soundtrack! Your love, strength, and support are invaluable to my entire life, thanks bae.

To my parents, Beverly Gibson and Robert Johnson (RIP) — you both instilled in me a deep love and honor for God — yes, Daddy, I "kept Jesus in the plan" and "perpetuated my gifts". You two also birthed in me a love for words and writing. Thank you, Ma, for being my unwavering support through some tough years, and for every prayer you prayed that I felt, but didn't know it was you. You will always be the Queen B to my Bumble Bee.

To my children, Kennedy and AJ, you two are my reasons for so many things I strive for in life. You all inspire me to be that example of tenacity, perseverance, and commitment needed to go far in this crazy world. Thank you for pushing me, nagging me, believing in me as I believe in you.

To my big brother, Craig (the best writer in the family), thank you for years of countless conversations mentoring me on the craft of writing. Every tool, resource, and strategy you shared was spot on and helped me grow. Consider this book my final project before I graduate to the next level of your lifelong writing masterclass.

To my book coach, Tiphani Montgomery, your Spirit-led November 2019 "Tell It" class opened the flood gates for me. I still can't believe how I tried to run from the class and wait until registration closed. Little did I know — I was dodging the final puzzle piece that would complete the strategy for this book. Thank you.

To my Sister Diamonds, Crystal Khalil and Dr. Nicole LaBeach, you two shined your light on me that day and lit a fire that accelerated my book labor. Frankly, that push to birth my purpose hurt so good, but that's what midwives do — discern when it's time to push and guide you through the delivery process. I appreciate your support, accountability, and willingness to hold space for my brilliance.

To my sis across the ocean (London), Angela Amadasun, who read this *book* while it was still a little ol' blog. You were my angel reader when I told this story, in real-time, as an anonymous blogger. And, we've been virtual sisters ever since, anonymous no more. Thank you, Ro (insider), for every kind word of encouragement, your prayers, and cheers.

To my "Sister Circle" and in loving memory of LaKita Garrett, you ladies have held me down and lifted me up in your own individual and collective ways too many times to list. I'm honored to call each of you my sister and so grateful for our community of women supporting and loving each other through every phase of our lives.

To my editor, Chonise Bass, you effortlessly caught the vision and direction for this work and made my manuscript sing! Thank you for moving, shifting, deleting, and challenging me. I'll always consider you as one of my brilliant play daughters from another mother.

Finally, to all of the *Someones*, those who God had in mind as He relentlessly pursued me to write this book, to "tell it", to share my testimony of overcoming childhood trauma and sexual abuse. God really, really loves you, and I'm honored to partner with Him to be a small part of your healing journey. Now, your healing happens.

Foreword

Free Women Free Women.

Is there any burden heavier for a child to bear than that of stolen innocence? Now, what if innocence were not the primary target nor intention? What if it were much more sinister, say, a flagrant act to defile and rob the human spirit?

Kim Bright's *Someone Borrowed, Someone Blue* is the journey and capture of a woman's voice once cloaked by trauma and sexual abuse. Her courage becomes a collective response to sexual trauma, speaking for those once sold an illusion of secrecy and unworthiness as the brand of their womanhood.

Throughout this work, Kim's voice perfectly aligns with that of the woman I call friend. When I met her, she stood with courage for me. I was wrongly accused and dishonored by the brokenness in another woman, and Kim used her voice to speak the truth, connect us by faith, and solidify my respect for her character. Some of the greatest friendships are born out of speaking up for another, giving a voice to a fellow sister who may not have one, or even recognizes they need one. I learned then that Kim Bright was a woman who chose principle over preference. She saw and chose the value of doing what was right despite the moment's discomfort, circumstance, or expectation. It's no surprise she was divinely chosen to birth *Someone Borrowed, Someone Blue*.

In this powerful epistolary of emails, two divinely connected strangers war against the mask of shame and proverbially speak the names of those who have experienced any form of trauma or sexual abuse. Through intimate conversation and revelation, Mikki Jones and Krystal Ashe form a bond that uncovers the path to fighting for one's soul. Their partnering of self-discovery and compassion bears witness to God's love and consummate ability to offer healing and wholeness beyond devastation. With each email, they move us beyond survival to an answered call to thrive. Their words take us on a journey of vulnerability and champion this most salient truth: **Free women free women**. When we abort our silence, tell our story, honor our light, and stand together, we not only free ourselves — we free each other.

Together they unveil a great irony, sexual assault is an act of terrorism that seeks to turn its victims into those who personally terrorize themselves. In their authenticity, we not only experience freedom from our pain, but freedom from the deception that ones' spirit could ever be stolen by an act of sexual violence. As Christ laid down his life, these women declare that attempts to rob a woman's spirit can only be achieved by one thing – Her own surrender.

For women seeking and celebrating freedom, *Someone Borrowed, Someone Blue* champions life beyond captivity and its promise of spiritual death. It is a brilliant labor of love. One that illuminates the power of warrior women to renew the broken heart and show it how to pump blood to itself first. Beyond expectation, it propels feeling, movement, and understanding to help us reclaim what's ours and accept an invitation to soar.

Dr. Nicole LaBeach
Master Relationship & Executive Coach
Co-Founder Sister Diamonds, LLC & TV Host on OWN's "Put a Ring On It"

Prologue

Draft saved Tue Jan 10, 2006 at 11:59 PM

This is crazy....

Draft saved Wed, Jan 11, 2006 at 12:11 AM

This is crazy.... What am I doing right now? Like, who could I send this to for help?

I

Sending Out an S.O.S.

Meanwhile, she found her contact information.
Just a general email address on
the Contact page of her website.
Good. She'd get her.
She's walked in her shoes before.
She's been where she is.
And quite frankly, she don't wanna be here no more.

Chapter 1

On Wed, Jan 11, 2006 at 11:11 PM Mikki Jones wrote:

Dear Ms. Ashe:

Hi. You don't know me, but I really need your help.

I read your book, *Like it Never Happened*, and I watched all your videos on healing from childhood trauma. I love your bluntness and transparency, and how you could explain exactly what I was feeling without even knowing me. After watching the video called, *"Your Healing is Possible — Even If You Don't Know How"*, I was in tears because I want so badly to heal, but no matter how hard I try, I still can't seem to shake the memories of my childhood sexual abuse.

The triggers keep popping up everywhere. I'm having nightmares. I'm biting everyone's head off. See, I had this thought that I could outrun them, you know? Put my mask on, and hide the pain from myself and others forever — but I'm completely exhausted. I spend most of my time at work locked in a bathroom stall so no one will catch me crying and start asking a bunch of dumbass questions. This is so ridiculous. I'm a grown, successful black woman just like you!

Now, I know you're a woman of faith, Ms. Ashe, and yes, I've tried to pray the pain away. I've even been asked, "Why ain't Jesus enough?" But what they don't realize is... how can I pray to God who allowed this mess to happen to me in the first place? This is driving me crazy and I don't think I can do this anymore.

Everyone else is too close, they won't understand. They're so judgmental. And church folk? They're the worse ones. They can be so ignorant of just how hard it can be when you're exhausted and trying the best you know how, and it still ain't good enough. I hurt so bad all over, all the time. I know you can relate to this level of pain — and at this point, I just want out!

So, if you don't help me, if this doesn't work, I just don't know. I feel so unworthy, ashamed, so foolish — and I have nobody to blame but my stupid self. It's all my fault!

I might as well just stop existing. Cos this here? This sure ain't living.

I am so tired. Please help me.

Mikki Jones

Chapter 2

On Thu, Jan 12, 2006 at 9:27 AM Krystal Ashe wrote:

Hi, Mikki!

Nice to meet you, and thank you for your email.

I appreciate you reaching out to me and trusting me with your words and how you're feeling right now. I must say the tone of your email has struck a chord in my heart. It was an SOS, sis, and you've got my attention.

I'm not quite sure what my help would look like from a distance, between my 2nd book tour and upcoming speaking engagements. But you know what? With God's very present help, I'm willing to try to help you wherever and however I can. And, I'll try to find some resources who can help you more so 1:1, OK?

Now. You said you can't shake the memories. I'm so sorry, Mikki. I truly understand how hard it can be to cope with the memories of childhood sexual abuse, molestation, trauma, etc.

If you've read my first book entitled, *Like it Never Happened*, you'll remember how after 30 years, I could *still* see and smell those two white boys. That's right. The ones who snatched me into those bushes at knifepoint on that hot summer day.

Sure, I was 5-years-old when it happened, but watch this: Even as a grown woman I couldn't shake the image of the one who had blond hair and a Shaun Cassidy haircut. The other boy behind me who had his hands over my mouth and a switchblade pressed to my neck — I don't quite remember his face much, but the smell of his dirty, sweaty hand is seared into my nostrils.

I remember being haunted by the blond boy who whipped out his wrinkly penis and then snapped the top of his jeans back. Let's just say the sight of his private part dangling like that outside his jeans was an image that a little girl in Kindergarten would never shake. As blondie was pulling my shorts off, I could only thank God for that random old white man who yelled, "Hey! You kids get out of there!"

Did you see what I did there, Mikki? The reality is there are some memories we will never forget, ever. That's what the brain does, it remembers.

But, here's the good news, sis — though the brain is only doing its job, we don't have to serve a life sentence in bondage to our memories either. The devil is a lie! God can heal your pain and brokenness, and restore your very soul like what? *Like it never happened* :).

So, before you go and try to *stop existing*, as you say, Mikki... can we try a few things, together?

Yours,
Krystal

Chapter 3

On Thu, Jan 12, 2006 at 9:50 AM Mikki Jones wrote:

OMG! THE Krystal Ashe? You answered?!

Wow. Just. I don't know what to say, thank you! I wasn't even sure if I had the right email address, or if you'd get my random email — let alone reply.

Something told me you of all people would understand. You know exactly what this trauma does to your mind, body — especially a woman's reproductive organs. Your TED Talk here in Atlanta last year was so true, how you tied the manifestation of unhealed trauma to fibroids. I'm battling fibroids and cysts as we speak. So, you already know how much I wish this shit had never happened to me. I should have approached you, said hello or something after that talk, but I didn't want to bother you.

My life from age 9 on would've been so much different... I feel so alone in this prison cell and really can't imagine what freedom even looks like.

Krystal, I want to be completely honest with you. Since I really didn't expect a reply, and so soon, I had already made plans to go away, to end this pain. The clinical depression, the pain and suffering, the torment would all be over. And, I found a way to make it look like an accident. Yep, got it all planned out. My husband and son would be taken care of with the insurance money. I even went as far as to pick the woman who should replace me as wife and mother...

But now? Now it looks like maybe I should give this healing thing one last try. So, if you're really willing to help me, maybe I can hang on a little while longer. But, I'm so ashamed...

You probably don't blame yourself anymore, huh? Sometimes, I feel so dumb. I'm angry at myself — why didn't I just tell that family member *no*? Or, why didn't I just say *stop*?

Then, other times, I remember why. I was so stupid and trusting in the fourth grade. I just didn't want to make my family mad at me because, well, they loved her soooo much. It was like they worshipped the ground she walked on. Shiiiit, I actually wanted and needed some of that love and attention they gave her. What was wrong with little Mikki?

So, I dunno. How could I have said no? How could I have said stop? If I would've told, she would've hated me. And if she didn't like me, NO ONE would love me. I would've lost what little acceptance I did have.

Am I wrong for wanting my family to love me like they *adored* her?

You do know... I was just as worthy of love, Krystal! Right? Yeah. Just as worthy. Maybe even more so.

Hell. I was blood.

Mikki

Chapter 4

On *Thu, Jan 12, 2006 at 3:20 PM Krystal Ashe wrote:*

Mikki,

Yes, love is your actual birthright. You were more than worthy to be loved back then — and that hasn't changed even now. Your worth is not tied to any kind of performance or anyone's evaluation of you. Because you are here, you're loved.

And of course, there were many, many times that I blamed myself, too, sis.

Why did I veer off and how in the world did I end up in those bushes? Why was I such a hard-headed little girl when the babysitter said "stay right outside this door"? Why was it so easy for those white boys to lure me away?

I eventually came to realize, Mikki, that it wasn't my fault. I did the best I could with the wisdom and knowledge of a 5-year-old — and so did you as a 9-year-old.

It may seem unimaginable right now, but you will get there, too. Everyone's healing journey is different, but with God's help, we all can land at a place that looks vastly different from the misery and bondage we've endured.

-Krystal

Chapter 5

On Thu, Jan 12, 2006 at 5:36 PM Mikki Jones wrote:

So, did you just get over it or pray your pain away? I'm a Christian, and I know that you're a woman of God, but churchy folk can be so judgmental, arrogant, and insensitive. They don't get just how hard it can be when you're on "E" and can't find the words to say, or do all the *churchy* things right...

When the painful memories strike the hardest, I'm usually too busy struggling to catch my breath from a panic attack, let alone pray and *war in the Spirit*, as some expect. Sometimes, I slip up. Too much alcohol, I eat too much. Sometimes there's no other way to describe what happened outside of the foul, 4-letter words that come to mind.

Can I keep it real and transparent with you, Krystal? Somedays, I can only mumble, "Jesus." Other days, 'Jesus' is followed by, "...this some f***** up s***!" God is gonna get me for that.

I sure hope no one else reads these emails, so embarrassing. I don't know what words will fly out of my mouth... I can't control the thoughts that are beating against my skull.

I'm just so angry at my life all the time. I can't help but think of all the happy, beautiful things I could be doing — but instead, I'm in my daggone 30's still dealing with this mess from the fourth grade. My existence looks nothing like the peace and abundance God promised. And now? It looks like I can't even get *Jesus* right.

I've just got some hard questions for God about this hellified situation. I mean, like... how in the world could God protect me from the bees, but not from this swarm of abuse that's eating me alive?

Mikki

Chapter 6

On Thu, Jan 12, 2006 at 10:58 PM Krystal Ashe wrote:

Your emails are safe with me, Mikki. No one else has access to this address but me — no one in my Houston or LA office, so it's ok.

I get what you're saying, sis. Nope, simply praying the pain away was not my experience. I wish it would have been; that would have been an easier fix than the years of therapy, blood, sweat, and tears it took to heal. And as far as your language is concerned, trust me, God has not changed His mind about His love for you, nor has He clutched any pearls about your words, your anger, or frustrations.

Don't get me wrong — God is all-powerful and our traumatic experiences don't overrule His authority. There are, however, some experiences in life that place two-ton boulders on our very souls, and freedom takes everything you've got — both spiritual and natural.

Funny you should say how hard it is to get your 'words right'. There was a period of time during my healing journey, say 2-4 years, where I couldn't find the words to say, either. And, by *say* I mean speak. Out loud. Coherent speech was a 'no' for me. My regular, everyday words

15

came out all jumbled. I ran to writing poetry and music because my tongue felt three inches thick and desert dry, girl. Probably because I was trying so hard not to let people see me sweat.

You ever get the sense that people can see, hear, or smell the trauma on you? Have you ever been afraid that you're reeking of your offenders' scent? So, you're running around and hiding from people so they won't find you out?

That was me, Mikki. It's crazy. Girl, I could be talking about some random topic, and out of the blue, my mind would have a flashback to those bushes. I'm talking no warning – wasn't even thinking about childhood. It would throw me all the way off and send me spiraling into a panic attack.

Funny not funny, there were other times when I, too, would be in meetings at work and would pretend like I had to use the bathroom. I'd excuse myself with some hard, fake cough like I needed a whole gallon of water LOL!

But in reality, sis, I was trying to beat my tears to the punch. For no good reason, those jokers were about to roll like a river down my face and across that conference room table. I was a professional in leadership at the time, no less. I couldn't let my colleagues see my ugly snot cry, the one I did at home on the bathroom floor with that one candle burning.

Do you remember in *Like It Never Happened*, how I talked about my old half bath downstairs across from the laundry room?

But wait, before I get into that, what are these *bees* you speak of? Tell me more. Are you allergic, sis?

CHAPTER 6

-Krystal

Chapter 7

On Fri, Jan 13, 2006 at 7:20 AM Mikki Jones wrote:

Hey Krystal,

Nawww... they're watching. Someone's always watching. Google employees, hackers...you do know that Al Gore's Internet isn't as safe as they want us to believe. I wake up paranoid every day that the unseen ones are reading all my stuff.

Anyway. That's good to know... I'm glad you don't expect me to just pray this pain away.

Cos if my prayers could reach heaven, if God was just a tad bit interested in a single one of my prayers — I wouldn't even need to have this conversation with *you* right now. Feel me?

But, I'll give Him credit. Somehow, God got it right with the bees. Nah, I'm not allergic. But, I still could've died that day. I'll never forget it.

It was that hot summer heading into the 3rd grade. Mama and I were driving home from her errands with all the windows open - girl, nothing but hot air circulating in the car. I didn't really mind; Mom believed you could save money on gas by not running the air conditioner as much. Single moms are always pinching pennies, right?

After a few miles in the heat, Mama said something that surprised me.

"Mik, roll up your window. I'm cutting the A/C on."

Huh? Well, it wasn't like I was about to argue with her. But, it was still a little strange. We're Florida girls, right? We know how to take the heat. Plus, we were only about 15 or so minutes from the house.

So, as I'm *manually* rolling up the window with that old school lever going around and around, I said,

"You sure, Ma? It's not that hot, I'm okay if you okay."

"No, let's go ahead a run a little A/C today."

Krystal Ashe, I lie to you not. Less than 5 minutes after we had all of the windows rolled up with the A/C blowing, a large black swarm-ball of bees hit our car! Girl, the car shook like a small bomb had hit it and Mama had to jerk the wheel to keep the car straight — we were riding across an overpass at the time of impact, no less!

You should've seen us, Krystal. Mama flipped on the windshield wipers and there were dead bees and bee juice streaks everywhere! There were so many bees that hit the car that bees started coming inside the car through the A/C vents! Mama had to turn the A/C off again.

I don't know how, but as all of this was going on, Mama never once pulled the car over. We were swatting, shutting vents, windshield wipers on high speed all while Mama maintained the car and we never got into an accident.

I remember after the initial impact, I glanced out of my passenger window and I saw this black, nebulous cloud of bees flying off into the sky.

I know this sounds like something from a movie, Krystal, but this is my real-life testimony. After having such a harrowing experience that day, I know that truly it had to be the Holy Spirit who whispered in my thrifty Mama's ears to wind up the windows and run her expensive A/C. I could only imagine what could have happened to us that day if God was not on watchful guard over us — with barely minutes to spare.

So yeah. I've experienced the protection of God. I give God the credit for saving our lives that faithful summer day. But to be honest, as my life went on and things took that turn, it left me baffled and searching for the answer to this question: *God, if you could protect me from those bees, where were you a year later ...*

-M

Chapter 8

On Fri, Jan 13, 2006 at 8:42 AM Krystal Ashe wrote:

Good lord, Mikki! I'm sitting here at my desk, sipping on my 2nd cup of coffee like...What a terrifying experience! To God be the glory!

I can imagine you and your Mom must've been scared out of your minds that day! I happen to hate bugs of any kind, and the thought of having my car covered in bees — while driving across an overpass —it makes my skin crawl (no pun), lawd!

Yes, girl, God deserves ALL the credit for keeping and protecting you that day. I'm so glad that your Mom listened to that still, small voice. I didn't always see it this way, but when God *whispers* to you, His voice is filled with love, guidance, and protection.

I learned this in my old half-bath downstairs across from the laundry room. It's the place where I first heard God's voice address the trauma (notice I didn't say "my" trama — here's a tip, never reference the trauma you've experienced from a position of ownership, it's not yours).

See, I was where you are now, Mikki, straight stressed out, crying for no reason, jacking up my words, snapping at my friends and family, and suicidal.

I would place a candle on the back of the toilet and pray to God, "*Lord, please help me.*" I didn't know what was going on with me, kinda. I say kinda because it was like I knew what was wrong, but I didn't want to admit the truth about what was wrong. It would cost too much and hurt too bad.

My strategy for 30 years had been to deny, deny, deny that what those white boys did to me broke me. I couldn't let them win. I pretended like it didn't phase me one little bit. Girl, I put that mask on, pranced around like I was all good. I never wanted anyone to smell their scent on my spirit — you know, that wet dog smell white people get when their dirty hair sweats? I didn't want people to see their filthy fingerprints across my mouth. So, I had to fake it. Until...

God finally whispered to me, audibly, on that bathroom floor, "*It's time for you to heal.*"

Sis, my mask was 30-years-old and glued to perfection like a lace-front wig. You couldn't tell where the mask began and where the real me ended. I was cool with that. But over time, life kept bumping into the mask, and I'd have to fix it back in place. Girl, you can't rock a lopsided mask, right? What's the point of that LOL?!

My real beef was that God was now taking His divine chisel and chipping away at my facade. He was about to uncover me. I was going to be exposed, and I was ugly and damaged. Honestly, Mikki? I thought that was the cruelest, most unfair thing God could ever do to me.

How dare He destroy a perfectly good cover-up after all these years? In my mind back then, sis, He should've just left well-enough alone.

To be honest, Mikki, it sounds like your mask is in the very same condition. I understand you're hurting but, with the right support, experience, and perspective, you can discover the truth about masks and where you really are. It's not what you think.

You can leave all the pain behind — without leaving — here.

Krystal

Chapter 9

On Fri, Jan 13, 2006 at 1:17 PM Mikki Jones wrote:

Well, my mask is cracked and on the ground in little pieces! It's beyond saving now. I feel so exposed. I'm out of hiding places.

And on top of all this mess, I can't seem to get people to love me right. Lord knows I have tried, even with everything that's going on inside me. You'd think folks would see your effort and give you some respect. If reciprocity was oxygen, I think I'd be dead by now.

I'm just tired, Krystal.

I can't keep fighting my demons while working for love and never getting any in return. What about me? What about all the sacrifices I make for others? I give, give, give and it's never good enough. It never has been...

Maybe I should just resign from life and love altogether.

-M

II

The Invitation to Heal

Do you really want to be free? Come on in!
The door's wide open. There's plenty of room.
Don't worry 'bout what to wear, what to bring,
or who else will be there.
Just RSVP 'Yes!' and come as you are.

I can't wait to see you.
I can't wait for you to
see the 'you' I see.

Chapter 10

On Fri, Jan 13, 2006 at 11:47 PM Krystal Ashe wrote:

Mikki, all of that frustration is telling you that it's time to heal and retire. You're right! Quit working for love, honey!

If it will help, write yourself a *"Dear love, I quit!"* letter. That's what I did. No two-week notice. No dramatic exit. Just up and quit. Full stop. Deuces! It was the one thing at the time that helped me to separate myself from an emotionally abusive and narcissistic marriage.

I had to be honest with myself. I wrote down all of the things I was doing for others so that they'd notice me, love me, honor me, appreciate me. Funny, not funny — the more you work for love, the more your pay gets cut! So what do co-dependent, people-pleasers like me do? We work even harder and we give even more!

Girl, before long, you're way below 'E' while everyone else is past 'F' — and STILL asking more of you. It's a mystery how folks who are engorged with your grace, kindness, and benevolence don't feel themselves about to pop! You are never enough to a narc.

Truth is, people recognize a sweet deal when they see it. Very few folks have the character or presence of mind to tell you to stop letting them use you. If you're waiting around for folks to say, "No, Mikki, stop giving me everything you've got while I don't even meet you halfway", sis, you'll be waiting forever. It has to start and end with you.

This whole journey does, my friend.

Mikki, are you ready to begin the journey to healing?

I think you are. I hear you and I understand that you feel like you're on your last leg. But, you also reached out to me. You still had enough sense to send out an SOS. That says a lot.

I get it. I know you feel like you want to die, but can we focus on that tiny part of you that really wants to live and be free?

Let's help her, please.

-Krystal

Chapter 11

On Sat, Jan 14, 2006 at 10:02 AM Mikki Jones wrote:

Yeah, I get it, Krystal. Cool. But, I've been thinking.

What if that tiny part of me that wants to be free is not strong enough?

What if the weight of the healing process crushes her? How can that tiny part of me carry the rest of me that's already planning my suicide?

I dunno, sis. Maybe this was a crazy mistake, you know, reaching out like this. I got my business all out in these emails. Anybody could hack us. There's probably folk we don't know reading this trail as we speak. Maybe I should just let sleeping dogs lie and let it go. Perhaps I'm just trippin' at the moment.

Why should I rile up all those old memories? Lord, I know what you're going to say. I heard you in one of your videos say *you can't heal what you won't face.*

Interesting. The more I think about it, you're gonna ask me to face the very thing that would push me over the edge, aren't you? How much

29

sense does it make to already be at a tipping point, and go messing around with the very thing that's going to send me to my grave?

M

Chapter 12

On Sat, Jan 14, 2006 at 6:51 PM Krystal Ashe wrote:

You're exactly right, Mikki. I can't and won't lie to you. Whether we like the truth or not, whether it feels good or hurts like hell — it's the truth.

So yes, sis, we have to face it to heal it.

But, I think you misunderstood what I meant when I said, "Let's help her, please."

I wasn't talking about you and me. "Let's" was not to imply that you and I would solve this problem together and heal you from this pain.

Those words were actually a *prayer to God.* A desperate, heart-felt petition to Him — not to you, love.

See, right now, I get it. You feel like two people on the inside — one who's tired, hopeless, and wants to die, and one who wants to be free from all this mess and live. And on any given day or at any given moment, you may want to die more than you want to live, and vice versa. And, while all this internal drama is going on, the devil wants you to believe that you're all alone, that no one will understand you — heck, he'll whisper that you might as well end it all, that death would be a welcomed reprieve from all the pain.

But here's the good news! I know a Great Equalizer who, if you just give Him space and permission, He'll take that tiny bit of strength you have left that wants to live and be whole, and He'll make up the difference with His strength so that you can begin to heal. God will carry you to victory when your heart wants to stop in defeat and you can't take another step. Girl, I'm a witness.

There's nothing on your healing journey that you'll have to face alone, Mikki. Jesus Christ himself and a host of angels will be there with you from start to finish, just like He was with me all those years. He's not the Alpha and Omega for nothing, girl.

You can do this, sis, and I'll still be here anytime you want to reach out and talk. OK?

May I send you a resource that can help?

-Krystal

Chapter 13

On Sun, Jan 15, 2006 at 6:42 AM Mikki Jones wrote:

Ok, Krystal. I dunno about this.

But, I'll try.

M

Chapter 14

On Sun, Jan 15, 2006 at 7:51 PM Krystal Ashe wrote:

Yay! Excellent, Mikki!

I'm so very proud of you, sis. Right now, you may not be able to recognize the power in this ONE baby step towards freedom, but you will.

Here's one of my best resources in Atlanta, give her a try. If you two don't click, I have a whole Rolodex of trusted providers.

Jamilah Jordan
Healing Happens
(404) 377-4325 (HEAL)

My 9-week book tour starts this Friday. First stop Miami, FL. Girl, do you see how God let us meet before things got crazy busy! I may be out of pocket from time to time — BUT I WILL RESPOND to your emails, no worries. And here's my personal cell 404-511-5683 for any urgent texts.

You are the one for whom my testimony was created, Mikki, and I honor God for bringing us together.

Praying for you, sis. Me, Jesus, and all of Heaven are rooting for you!

Let me know how it goes. I'm here.

Yours,
Krystal

Chapter 15

On Mon, Jan 16, 2006 at 1:12 AM Mikki Jones wrote:

Thank you so much, Krystal. I can't find the words right now to express my appreciation, but hopefully, one day I will.

Yep, I'm down with that one, little baby step. Just look at what one little email did :).

I'll give Ms. Jordan a call this week and tell her you sent me. Let you know how it goes.

Thank you for being here, Krystal. I really need someone to understand where I'm coming from. Someone who wouldn't judge me for my pain and frustrations. Someone who was strong enough to let me borrow their strength in my emotional, mental, and physical exhaustion.

I really do thank God for you. Welp, let's see where this goes...

-M

Chapter 16

On Tue, Jan 17, 2006 at 8:15 AM Krystal Ashe wrote:

Excellent! My pleasure, sis.

Krystal

III

Start Right Here

Begin again. This time, without rewind.
Your move — and only your move — counts.

Chapter 17

On Thu, Feb 9, 2006 at 12:40 PM Mikki Jones wrote:

Hey Krystal!

How are you, sis? How's the book tour coming along?

Sooo guess what?

Yeah, I like her. I'm still kinda on the fence about how I'm going to reach this invisible finish line, but Jamilah is a keeper. I had my intake appointment yesterday — at her swanky, new office — and wanted to let you know how it went.

So yeah, Jamilah has a very gentle spirit, very motherly. Her calm, welcoming smile when I met her disarmed me. She has the kind of personality that melts all of your defenses away, doesn't give you any reason to resist. To be honest, that made me nervous. Shooot, I was prepared for a fight — girl, don't ask me why. Part of me wasn't sure if I should trust it, but the other part of me really wanted to fall like a pile of Dominos at her feet and just cry. I dunno. The session made a lot of emotions and thoughts run through my head.

I can dig the aura of her office, though. It's painted with vibrant colors, and she has theeee best smelling candles burning. Girl, I can tell she spent some money on those candles. I love quality candles.

I used what strength I had to be real open and honest with her. Thankfully, I didn't feel any judgment from her, which is cool because I didn't need her to tell me how dumb I was. I already know I should've known better. Every 9-year-old on the planet knows that family members shouldn't be performing sexual acts on them and that if they share porn with you, that's the devil. I don't care how much you love them. I was just dumb and stupid.

Anyway, I'll tell you what I appreciated the most — her work with women who are experiencing gynecological issues. Her expertise with fibroids on a holistic healing level is an extra bonus — you definitely checked that box, Krystal.

If I can get rid of these things and get over this abuse crap — wow, what a miracle that would be. My periods have gotten to the point where the pain is unbearable. On Day 1, I'm in the bed for at least 6 hours (yeah, I timed it) with excruciating pain in my lower back that shoots down my right leg. And, it's really gross but, I'm passing clots the size of chicken gizzards! Girl, I thought I was dying in the shower the other day, seeing huge clumps of bloody matter plop right onto the shower floor. I thought my liver was coming out of me in small pieces! Had a full-on panic attack.

I know, TMI. But as a fibroid survivor yourself, I trust you can relate.

Jamilah says, "Healing happens", so we will see. I'll keep you posted.

Still can't thank you enough for taking the time to help a total stranger. Others would have clicked "Delete". You see hope and deliverance. I have hopeful moments here and there when I want to see deliverance, too.

We'll see.

Bless,
M

Chapter 18

On Sun, Feb 12, 2006 at 10:37 PM Krystal Ashe wrote:

Wonderful, Mikki! So proud of you!

Through all the pain and exhaustion you're experiencing, you found the strength and courage to take a major step towards your healing.

Nobody could do this for you, Mikki. YOU had to do it for yourself. Major props, sis! How you view your identity, your belief system, how you respond to this season of your life — let's just say it's all about to drastically change.

So yeah, Jamilah is one of my top resources and a champion for women who are experiencing gynecological issues like fibroids, cysts, endometriosis, etc. Her holistic approach to healing is amazing. She'll definitely connect the dots for you because there's a deep correlation between what we think and how our thoughts manifest in our physical bodies, especially for women.

I want you to stay encouraged, Mikki. Right now, your finish line may seem invisible, as you say, but just because you can't see it off in the distance, doesn't mean it's not there. Believe me when I tell you, sis, you will get over this and finish stronger than you can even imagine right now.

You'll find out soon enough that you are more than what 'they' did to you.

And don't dare leave Jesus at home, sis. Take Jesus with you to counseling! With God's help and Jamilah's guidance, you'll find the strength to do your work, confront the root of every issue, and surrender to the healing process. You're in both good spiritual hands with God and natural hands with Jamilah.

The book tour is off to a super start, thanks for asking. *"Renouncing Victimhood"* is resonating with so many people across the country. It was so hard to write (and actually do), but God is blessing its impact. Next stop, New York!

Yours,
Krystal

Chapter 19

On Fri, Feb 24, 2006 at 2:48 PM Mikki Jones wrote:

Hey Krystal,

Amazon delivered my copy of *Renouncing Victimhood* today. Very cool sky blue cover art, sis.

I won't dive in head first right now. I think this 2nd book will be a bit challenging for me at the moment, you know, with the title and all. But, I definitely wanted to support you nonetheless.

I did scroll the Table of Contents, though. And that Introduction? "*I was born with a toe tag on standby. Standard procedure for stillborn babies, even if only precautionary.*" Sis, you sure do have a way with words LOL!

Can't wait to read the chapters where you talk about your struggles: people-pleasing, young promiscuity, porn addiction, etc. But, I'll have to come back to that whole section on forgiveness, especially given the homework Jamilah gave to me.

From the looks of the video and press coverage, the book tour is going well. I'm so happy for you; you deserve it, Krystal. Maybe when I get myself together I can go on tour with you, you know, just as a living witness of your testimony and your dedication to support other women. I dunno... I'm just talkin'.

Anyway, Jamilah gave me my first real assignment during my session last Wednesday. It's something called the *Forgiveness Diet*. For 7 days straight, I have to spend 20-minutes in the morning and 20-minutes at night before bed writing statements like: "I, Mikki, forgive _____ for _____ totally and unconditionally." Girl, I told her I'm a follower of Jesus and ain't no way she gon' get me to tell lies 40 minutes a day for a whole week LOL! She fell out laughing with me.

But, seriously, inside I kept thinking "is this for real?" I'm really not feeling it, to be honest. Forgive totally and unconditionally? Girl, where they do that at?! Oh, a sista got some conditions, alright!

I mean, how much sense does it make to let people who hurt me get away scot-free? They were the ones who did *me* wrong, and I'm just supposed to gift wrap them a laminated "get out of jail free" card?

It doesn't seem right and it sure ain't fair - not given all the years I've suffered from the memories, the flashbacks, the nightmares, dysfunctional relationships, the panic attacks.... Good Lord.

Sigh. Jamilah has convinced me that I can trust her, so I'm going to try and trust this crazy process. I start this Monday, finish Sunday. We'll review the following Wednesday at the next session. Jamilah says she has a whole graduation ceremony planned for me. This should be interesting, we'll see.
Chat later,

M

Chapter 20

On Sat, Feb 25, 2006 at 6:17 PM Krystal Ashe wrote:

Hey there, Mikki!

Here at LaGuardia waiting on a delayed flight — girl, your email makes the wait worth it; well, almost. I am so ready to get in my own bed!

THANK YOU so much for your support, Mikki. Really praying that my words help another woman — or man — to overcome and defeat the monsters of sexual abuse and childhood trauma, but also the monster called Victimhood.

Girl, you can read *Renouncing Victimhood* straight through, skip around, use the book however you'd like when you are ready. I understand the subject matter and call to action may be a little overwhelming right now. The book is really the next step or Part 2 after God heals you "like it never happened."

Now, I don't want you to freak out, but — healing requires maintenance; it takes work to *get* free AND *stay* free. Renouncing victimhood is the part of healing that helps overcomers stay free.

When you do read it, I want you to make it yours and zoom in on the parts that you need when you need them. Everyone heals differently, but most, if not all, begin their healing with a healthy dose of forgiveness.

Lord, the Forgiveness Diet... sis, I'm all too aware LOL.

I can remember it like it was yesterday. I went out and bought a nice, shiny new 5-subject notebook; it was yellow with college ruled lines, and I loaded up on some pens. Girl, I had some serious forgiving to do. I didn't know if only one notebook and 20-minutes day and night were going to be enough space and time for me. I even had the nerve to ask if I could just type all those sentences from my laptop LOL!

At that time, if I could've laid eyes on those white boys, even at 35, I would've tried to kill 'em with my bare hands — yeah, I know, dramatic. But real. At best, I'd want to press some kind of charges. But I think the statute of limitations was at zero after 30 years. So I wasn't feeling the whole "totally and unconditionally" thing either. It will be a process, Mikki, and I'm sure you're going to make your way through it next week.

Just be honest and true with all that you're feeling. I'm sure you've already been told this, but don't judge or limit who or what comes to mind. Wanna know something? Here I thought it was an exercise to help me overcome the trauma, but I found myself writing down things I had held in my heart against my elementary school teacher, this football player in junior high who called me "pretty but ugly, too" at a pep rally, a homegirl who I felt betrayed me in college — I mean once I got in the flow, everyone started coming out of the woodworks like roaches LOL! I had no idea all the crap I was holding on to. It was a lot, every single day for 7 days, forgiving this, forgiving that.

But always remember what I told you last month. One of the greatest tricks the devil will play on you is convincing you that you're all alone. He'll lie and tell you that no one else understands what you're going through because your story is so unique — it's not. He'll play on your weakness and tell you you're dumb for doing things that will make you hurt more or cry harder. The enemy will manipulate you and tell you that you're actually going backward — and it will feel like that for a season. And then he'll blame God for tricking you into believing that getting help and facing the pain was the "right" thing to do.

Listen to me good. Don't you for 1-second focus on his foolishness, Mikki. It's all lies from the pit of hell. Nope, healing ain't pretty and it ain't easy either. But it will be worth every tear you cry, every ache in your heart, and every ounce of forgiveness rung out of your soul to be free.

You're off to a great start, and God who has begun this amazing work in you is more than able to see you through to reach the finish line. Trust Him and the process, k?

Prayers,
Krystal

IV

Forgiveness is a Dirty Job

*The pain and trauma must be sacrificed
on the altar of surrender.
Those twins won't go willingly.
Things are about to get messy.*

Sometimes, you have to make a mess to clean up a mess.

Chapter 21

On Sat, Mar 4, 2006, at 6:26 AM Mikki Jones wrote:

Thank you, Krystal. You just don't know what your encouragement means to me.

It's the morning of Day 6. Two more days of this. Girl, my handwriting has turned into kindergarten chicken-scratch. My fingers are achy, and I'm pretty exhausted with all of this forgiveness day and night stuff. But, I know if I miss 1 day, if I miss 1 morning or night session, I'd have to start the whole 7-day process all over again. Those are the rules. And ain't no way in the world I'm going back to Day 1. I'm almost at the finish line — well, *this* particular finish line at least.

You were right, Krystal. Spending time alone with my thoughts, combing through my mind to forgive folks... yeah, a lot of random people have shown up outside of that family member — heck even my Mama. To be honest, after holding on to these hurts for so long, and being a more mature woman now, I don't even know if they knew how I felt or if what I've been hurting about was even real.

Many of my "forgiveness sentences" are what I thought about a situation that happened a long time ago. It's been all in my mind, but I honestly never confronted the other person. I've just been mad. Angry. Holding on to it. Some things I would never say out loud to the person anyway. A lot of my offense feels kinda petty or I feel embarrassed about the way I feel. But I honestly felt it no less, so like Jamilah said, I won't judge myself for it. I guess writing all this stuff day and night is at least helping me to put it all on paper and see it outside of myself.

I will say it's definitely been easier to write about all that crap my family member did to me than to confront them about it. I could never find the courage to look her in the eyes and say it to her face. But it's on paper now, and that will have to do. Having 7 days to write and write... I broke the molestation down into tiny pieces, writing forgiveness statements for everything she did — every way she looked at me, everything she said to me, the introduction to porn at 9, the shower — everything I thought she thought or did or saw or said. It all has a forgiveness sentence now. It's all right there in blue ink, out of my head, and between the lines of pages and pages of notebook paper.

Well, I'd better get started on my 20-minute morning session. I can't wait to turn this assignment into Jamilah tomorrow. She said she has something special planned. We'll see.

Ever have your heart feel a little bit lighter, but your mind was still heavy?

Just a lot of emotion, this is hard.

M

Chapter 22

On Tue, Mar 7, 2006, at 10:38 PM Mikki Jones wrote:

Krystal! Guess what! Ok, long email alert...

I made it through, sis, whoop whoop! Assignment complete. No more forgiveness sentences to write! I was so happy to hand that notebook to Jamilah like, "Girl, take it! You can have it!"

I thought the hard part was over. That is until she told me what came next...

For the session, we actually moved to her sea-blue room. This room had a hand-painted mural of a woman in an Egyptian blue gown, kneeling in aqua-blue water with both of her hands lifted toward a cloudless blue sky with a big, yellow sun-circle above her head. The whole scene was beautiful. She was in full-on surrender as she knelt behind Jamilah. Sitting directly in front of Jamilah, I would often glance up at the woman, kinda envious of her strength in surrender.

Nothing and no one could prepare me for what I experienced next.

It was time for my forgiveness graduation ceremony... and oh my Lord.

Jamilah explained the format. I would now *verbalize* some of my hardest forgiveness sentences. Krystal, I thought I was going to pass out or run outta that room. See, it was one thing to be able to sit alone quietly, think in my head, and write down my thoughts of forgiveness on paper.

Now, I had to speak it out loud. I had to imprint the atmosphere with my voice. A voice I had long lost, never speaking about the trauma to anyone but my BFFs and my husband only less than a year ago prior to this night.

And remember, I'm in a state where I can't find verbal words right now anyway! I was struggling, trying to convince Jamilah that this was a bad idea and that I liked writing better. I tried so hard to reason with her to the point where I felt my throat tightening up, like when you're about to cry. She wasn't trying to hear any of it. So much for those efforts...
So, there I was. Jamilah explained that there was power in my verbal, audible words. I knew this from the Bible, but I didn't have the strength or know-how to apply that scripture to *this* part of my life. I probably didn't even want to.
It was time for the ceremony to begin. Jamilah gave me the instructions.

Ok. I was to look Jamilah in the face and say the name of the person I was forgiving and what I was forgiving them for. Lord Jesus! There was no limit to what I could say, and I could repeat the same name over and over if needed.

Once I was done, what came next broke me down even more.

Jamilah would respond AS THAT PERSON — for example, "Mikki, please

forgive me for (whatever I said), I'm sorry for hurting you when I
_____. I apologize."

We began.

I made it through the first few names and offenses. Jamilah pushed
me to go deeper. That's when tears started to flow and I could feel my
stomach balling up in a hard knot.

Name after name.
'Please forgive me, Mikki when I ...'
Next name.
'Mikki, I'm sorry I ....'
Next name.
'Mikki, please forgive. I apologize for ....'

By this time, I'm nauseated, sweating profusely, and trying hard not
to let my nose drip. I didn't know if I had the strength to finish the
graduation ceremony. From childhood to adulthood, I was almost out
of names.

I knew good and well whose name was left. Just one. Hers.

I could feel my heart beating out of my chest to the point where my
skin pulsed everywhere. And by this time, I was writhing in the chair,
pulling on my hair and clothes like a crackhead who needed a fix. It was
pretty ugly.

I said her name and thought I would vomit in my lap. The room started
spinning like a merry-go-round; I couldn't make the lady on the wall
be still. I could feel my throat closing up for good. In my mind, I was

screaming "Jesus!", because surely the devil and at least 5 of his imps had their hands wrapped around my throat trying to strangle me.

But, I had come this far. Seven days of forgiveness day and night. Thousands of words on notebook paper. I remembered you saying that God was more than able to see me through to reach the finish line. You said God promised to be my Omega. I thought to myself "*You promised me, God, so...*"
I half-mumbled the first offense like, "*How could you...*" The second. The third.

Then, the flood gates opened. Through an ugly snot cry, I poured and poured what those events had done to me as a child, and how they affected me as an adult — how used and inferior they made me feel, how fearful of women I became, how my worth as a human was only tied to sexual prowess, how I felt shame, and blame, and isolation with this secret — till I got it all out.

There. I said it. It was all out. It was all gone.

Jamilah graciously took her time and let all of the words I yelled at her hang in the air until I'd calmed down a bit.

Then, with the sincerest facial expression I'd seen all night, Jamilah looked me square in my bloodshot eyes and said, "Mikki, I am eternally sorry for what I did to you. Please forgive me for.... "

She addressed every point I made; she didn't miss one offense.

Krystal, I was broken. Just done.

It took a while for me to gather myself together, sip some water, and return to normal breathing. To be honest, I was kinda embarrassed to go through all of those emotions in front of someone, but I also felt relieved and grateful that Jamilah was such a graceful, gentle counselor.

After the verbal exercise, we went outside to the back deck of her offices. Covered by a red-orange sky at sunset, we burned the pages of my notebook.

It was finished. The flames crawled across every heartache; every pen stroke of pain and brokenness disappeared, consumed by the fire. Each offense burned from red to black smoke, the pages unrecognizable. The words were gone. Ashes tossed in the garbage where they belonged all my life.

I felt like a newborn baby, sis. That was some good ol' sleep that night.

Just grateful.

Mikki

Chapter 23

On Fri, Mar 10, 2006, at 7:37 PM Krystal Ashe wrote:

Wow, Mikki. Just, wow!

Happy graduation, sis! They say the *Forgiveness Diet,* and subsequent forgiveness graduation, is one of the hardest mental and emotional healing experiences to navigate. It really sets you up and gives you a firm foundation from which to leap into your healing process.

Yes, my sister, this is the beginning of the process, and now you can move forward a little lighter and a little freer than before.

The important thing I want to ask is: can you see what's possible now? Can you imagine yourself living free from the pain and trauma?

See, what unforgiveness does is it acts as a filter to block the light of freedom. Harboring all of those ill feelings makes the possibility of healing seem so far-fetched and the chance of being a 'new you' ridiculous and silly.

If you hold on to the past and keep reliving the hurt and pain, you'll never have any time left to live in a free and healed present.

The pain and resentment will block your healing and make it so you can't see yourself living forward without it. Those crackhead withdrawals you had were real, girl. And that's what you must now begin to learn to do — live forward without the bitterness, without the pain that had embedded itself deep in your very soul.

You became your pain and trauma. It was a seamless part of your identity. How do I know?

Because my trauma was deeply rooted in my personality, too. It was 'who I am'. I became the living embodiment of the stench of molestation versus, simply, molestation happened to me. I spoke the language of MY molestation, MY sexual violence, MY attempted abduction. I owned it. It was mine. And in many instances, I gave it energy like I loved and cared for it. I protected that horrible experience from anything and anyone who would try to take it away from me. It was mine.

I had to learn to let it go. I had to learn that I didn't need it anymore to be Krystal, and that was a process.

Now you're a graduate, Mikki. What was once "yours" has gone up in flames. The rising smoke has carried away every offense and painful event that caused you heartache, nightmares, and tears.
The challenge ahead? Let the ashes remain ashes. Girl, don't you dare go sifting through the ashes in your mind to find those past hurts you just forgave.

Don't go trying to glue ashes together to revive that monster of depression and pain. You want to let the smoke go, sis! No pet smoke, and don't pet the smoke lol!

And whatever you do, don't be like me — putting a lid on the smoke to keep it contained in my head, so I can tap the glass every now and then lol. Somebody say, "Krystal! Step away from the smoke!"

You've experienced a personal rebirth. Selah. And, so it is! Now, allow yourself to be born, again! This time the way God intended, how God saw you... loved, beautiful, and whole.

Krystal

Chapter 24

On Fri, Mar 24, 2006 at 12:22 AM Mikki Jones wrote:

Hey Krystal.

I kinda hear you.

But, if God really saw me that way from get-go — loved, beautiful, whole — why did He allow this trauma to ever happen to me?

I was only 9, so I know I couldn't have done that much wrong in that short amount of time to need to be punished, taught some cruel lesson. I don't understand that part.

The loaded, 'elephant in the room' question, Krystal, is this: Where was God?

If everyone's forgiven now, slate clean, smoke gone — then who's left to own responsibility? Everyone keeps saying, including Jamilah, "It wasn't your fault, Mikki." Cool. OK. I'm starting to believe them. Kinda.

But, whose fault was it? Things happened to me. Why?

Sis, I know that I'm just learning how to crawl in my new life of forgiveness, but something is still off. It seems as though I forgot to add someone's name to my forgiveness diet...IJS.

M

Chapter 25

On Mon, Mar 27, 2006 at 12:29 PM Krystal Ashe wrote:

Hey Mikki,

I'm finally home-sweet-home at last! Can't wait to share more about how God showed out on the book tour these past months. Remind me to give you a recap... But for now, let's talk about what you're feeling. It's painfully and personally familiar, sis. I'll share how I navigated these thoughts and emotions. Here's my long email alert :)...

First, your rationale is both fair and accurate — you're exactly right, someone IS missing. There it is. Learning to crawl in order to walk in forgiveness' shoes is 'bout to get even more real.

Remember how you were tormented at your forgiveness graduation, squirming in your chair by the mere mention of *her* name? Sis, the same thing happened to me. But, not when I said the words, *"white boys"* — but when I said the word, *"God"*.

How could I ever forgive God? And, why was God crashing my forgiveness graduation?

I was a kid, only 5. To be snatched and dragged into those bushes with a knife to my neck — how in the world could a God so loving and kind, the One to whom I proclaimed my love and devotion, how could He allow me to be treated like I was trash, like I was nothing?

And worse yet, I have a daughter. How in the world could I trust God to protect her in this evil world, if He wouldn't even protect me?

Where was I to put Psalm 91? Did Psalm 121:7, *"The Lord will protect you from all evil"*, not apply to me? Only to God's *special* children? Did God have the whole world in His hand — but somehow, oops, drop me? Did He lose sight of me in the thick brush? Hold up! Aren't His eyes in every place watching the evil and the good?

All of these thoughts ran through my head, too, Mikki. I totally get it.

While nothing about mental and emotional healing from trauma happens overnight, I had to be willing to begin the process by forgiving all — including God.

In my *expert* assessment, if anyone could've stopped the events on that dreaded day — it was God — and He didn't. But now I had to forgive Him. I had to let God off the hook for something I believed He clearly didn't use His power to prevent. I thought God let me down, and I was really angry and hurt about it.

So, how did I do all of that?

Well, the first hard thing I had to do was accept and acknowledge my proper position and order.

I had to relinquish my imaginary throne that sat higher than God. Even in all of my unquestionable, justified hurt and pain, who was I to position myself above my Creator and call Him to repent to me before my throne? Sis, we're talking about the Creator of the whole, entire Universe — within which, I am merely a speck. God had to answer to me? I had unsettled beef with Him?

Yep. I'd found Him guilty as charged. I proudly sat (out of place, of course) as both His judge and jury. I got to the point where I'd rejected hearing any eyewitness testimony of His goodness and mercy. And, I overruled all presentations of evidence that would prove God's innocence.

That is... until I had my *Job moment.*

Mikki, one day I took a break from railing against God — guess you could say it was a good day, a day for God to catch me off my guard. I was reading my Bible, and ran across Job 30:20-21 (MSG):

*"I shout for help, God, and get nothing, no answer!
I stand to face you in protest, and you give me a blank stare!
You've turned into my tormenter—
you slap me around, knock me about.
You raised me up so I was riding high
and then dropped me, and I crashed.
I know you're determined to kill me,
to put me six feet under.*

Girl, finally! Someone understood where I was coming from; Job felt the same way I did! I had to keep reading, sis, because I wanted to hear what God had to say for Himself LOL! Hmmph, causing an innocent, righteous man like Job to suffer. Job lost much more than I had. Let's be real now, my complaint was valid — but Job had an entire lock on pain and misery.

So, as I continued reading in my bed, surrounded by empty Twizzler wrappers, wine bottles, and tear-soaked pillows, I heard an audible rip in my spirit.

It was my judge's robe.

It was being torn. Word after word, chapter after chapter, I was being stripped, and there was nothing I could do to fight it. I was not only being dethroned, I found myself being escorted to the Divine Court of the true and living God. I was summoned to take the witness stand and answer for my poor behavior.

And I, like Job, couldn't find the answers to God's questions anywhere. At least, none that would make any good sense. God said,

"In all of your honor, wisdom, and majesty, Krystal Ashe, I have some questions for you. And, you must answer them. Brace yourself like a woman:

- Where were you, Krystal Ashe, when I laid the foundations of the earth and its measurements (Job 38:4-5)?
- When's the last time you, Krystal Ashe, commanded the morning to appear or caused the dawn to rise in the east (Job 38:12)?
- Do the hawks take flight by your wisdom, Krystal Ashe, or do the eagles soar at your command (Job 39:26-27)?
- Do you have arms like Me, Krystal Ashe? Can your voice, Krystal Ashe, thunder like Mine (Job 40:9)?

- Can you, Krystal Ashe, bring any valid claim against Me when I own everything in heaven and under heaven (Job 41:11)?"

Lord. Every verse felt like machine gun bullets hitting me center mass, ripping through my pride and bitterness. I know that sounds dramatic, but I was so shameful and remorseful, Mikki. Had I really tried to stand toe-to-toe with God and challenge Him like that?

I didn't want any more of this.

God pulls your coat tail like, "Ummm Ma'am, okay. Your tantrum is over." — and let's just say I had a total shift in my attitude and perspective. I stopped looking at all of the facts and started looking at the truth that there's a difference between *causation* and *allowance*.

See, there were deep-rooted elements to my anger against God — as if He *caused* the trauma. In my mind, because He allowed it, He must've orchestrated it. Trauma can really shift your thinking to the left, especially when you're in a position to rightfully blame others for your pain.
But thankfully, God didn't leave me there in a pile of shame and remorse. He then began to show me His loving hand in the middle of a horrible situation.

He showed me where He was in my situation. I could've been stabbed, throat slit, penetrated, beaten, killed — but God broke up the event when that old white man saw us and shooed us from the bushes. He yelled, "What are you kids doing in there!" The man thought we were intruding around his property. The white boys let me go and ran. Somehow, I found my way back to the sitter's house, where I acted like it never happened.

Mikki, I don't know how God will reveal Himself to you in your situation, but I do encourage you to stop, take a deep breath, and listen to Him. Drop the charges against God. Release Him from your self-validated indictment, trial, and guilty verdict.

You can rail against God and resist Him but for so long. Our pain will never crack His loving, divine nature. By the mere fact that we're having this convo, I believe that God is at work, massaging your heart, healing every place in your relationship with Him that's been fractured by your pain and disappointment.

Perhaps if only to show you His loving, healing power to restore. That one day, you may share with others as I have shared with you :-).

Krystal

Chapter 26

On Mon, Apr 24, 2006 at 9:53 AM Mikki Jones wrote:

Hey Krystal,

So, just got back a couple of weeks ago from Spring Break with the family. It was such a much-needed vacation in FL with some family time. Sometimes you need a break from the "work" of healing. You do know this is some shonuff work, right LOL?! I needed that break. I do miss Jamilah, though. I'll see her again this Wednesday.

All the while in Miami, I kept reading your last email over and again. Forgiving God... geesh. I spent some quiet time at the beach alone listening to the voice of God. It's like I can hear Him speaking through the ocean waves. I don't know about you, sis, but the beach does a sista some good — both emotionally and spiritually.

All I kept saying to myself was "wow". That God interrogation! Whew, that was some real serious stuff you experienced in order to forgive God. I guess God told you LOL! Jk!

But seriously, God has a way of getting our attention eventually and bringing us back to reality. It hasn't been easy, but over the last few sessions, I've been working to release God — while making sure I don't continue to indict myself. That's a very intricate balancing act. But I'm learning to navigate my way through it.

I'm still growing through feeling like someone has to take full responsibility for what happened. I'm not strong enough to confront my family member, I don't think I ever will be. So there's that. I can't blame her to her face. I'm learning not to blame God anymore. Jamilah says I am not to blame. Man. There are times when I still struggle with "everyone got off scot-free". Traumatic events happened with a ripple effect on my entire life and no one's been punished for it. Got it. ~~Cool~~? Not cool...

I'm seeing now how my Forgiveness Diet and graduation ceremony were not the finish line, but simply my springboard — a foundation to jump-start my healing. That was kinda genius of Jamilah. Now, I gotta keep standing. At first, it felt like quicksand, but somehow these ankles are getting stronger :).

M

V

Masks Won't Hide You From Your Secrets

Well, would'ya look at that. There you are, again!
Wherever you go, you are always there.

Chapter 27

On Tue, May 2, 2006 at 3:46 PM Mikki Jones wrote:

Hello there, Krystal!

Well, whaddya know LOL! Guess what I found out last week in my session... You've been holding out on a sista!

I dunno if Jamilah let it slip out or if she wanted me to know — but she told me that I reminded her of you and that if healing could happen for you, it could definitely happen for me, too! She sees how much I talk about you, how appreciative I am of you being a safe place and confidant for me. When I "grow up" and out of this mess, you already know who I want to be like LOL!

It hit me one day that you didn't just give me one of your 'top counselor resources' from your extensive database. Girl, you gave me your personal therapist, the person who guided you to freedom. Man. You gave me, a total stranger, your very best.
You didn't have to do that, Krystal, but I am sooo grateful that you did. I'm coming along slowly, but surely. And I'm definitely in better shape than the day I sent you that first email. So grateful.

I saw your talk online at that women's conference in Dallas last week. Hope your next speaking engagement rocks the house as always. Thanks for sharing your appearance schedule on your website. It allows me to keep up and say a quick prayer for you on the road with the book tour. I see you rising on Amazon... go, girl!

You're helping a lot of people, sis. Be sure to get some rest here and there, till next time.

Mikki

Chapter 28

On Thu, May 11, 2006 at 10:02 PM Krystal Ashe wrote:

Ha! You got me, Mikki LOL! That Jamilah is something else. You needed someone who could get results. I would've told you how close we were, but I didn't want you to feel like I was pressuring you. Or, if you two weren't a good fit, I didn't want you to feel any kind of way to say, "Nahh, she ain't it."

Your healing is what's important to me, Mikki — not so much who God chooses to guide you there. I'm a firm believer that for the one seeking healing, who they feel comfortable with is what matters, period. You and only you decide that. But yes, Jamilah was a winning counselor for me, too. Girl, I'm so glad you two hit it off — if you could've seen my exhale, whew .

Jamilah came into my life at the recommendation of a friend. It's funny, I even told my friend that I was scouting counselors for another friend LOL!

Yeah, I was faking the funk, but that's what we do when our lives are being choked by shame. Funny how we often protect our masks and our personas to a greater degree than our own mental health.

Speaking of, are you seeing now that masks are the very things that block our freedom? They're not real. They only exist in the pseudo-reality of strength and "unbotheredness" that we've created for ourselves.

I remember when it started to make sense for me... how could God ever heal a mask? Or, how can God heal personas that don't really exist?

Mikki, every time we touch base, you're showing signs that your masks are broken. I know you still feel exposed, vulnerable like someone snatched all of your clothes off and you're standing in the middle of the busiest mall naked. Girl, do I know the feeling!

I say all that to say that I actually do pray that God continues to crack open that hard shell — the masks that have kept you from your healing all these years.

You're doing just fine right where you are, at your own pace, sis. Keep going!

Krystal

Chapter 29

On Fri, May 19, 2006 at 1:46 AM Mikki Jones wrote:

Krystal,

Smh girl. That sure is an accurate description of what I feel right now. I'm straight up standing butt-naked in this mall of life, and no amount of squirming and hand covering can hide my shame from folks. It sucks.

It's like all of my twisting and turning to hide my 'private parts' at every angle has actually drawn more attention to myself. As much as I wish people would mind their own business and do their shopping lol, I'm actually the one shining a spotlight on myself with my snappy attitude, outbursts, or just plain silence with zero emotion.

Not only can everybody see my shame, they now know I was hiding something all along. They know I was a fake and a phony. That I didn't have it all together as I led them to believe. I did need help. I did need them. Sometimes, that part hurts worse than the actual shame.

So, I'll be working all of this out in my upcoming sessions. Jamilah says the next leg of my healing journey will include the people who matter to me the most. Scary. When I heard this, I could've put money on Jamilah starting me out with the one person closest to me at the time of the trauma — my Mama. Lord, this is gonna be a trip.

Jamilah says an important part of healing from childhood trauma, child sexual abuse, etc. is often a loving and honest conversation with our parents. To be real honest, I don't know about all this.

Sis, it's been over 25 years. I know Jamilah doesn't think I have the strength to expose these secrets and tell my Mama what happened now! I mean, what good would that do anyway — other than stress my Mama out over old news she can do nothing about.

Mama probably wouldn't believe me. Nah, on second thought, I know she would believe me. It's just that I'd be asking her to believe the unbelievable. We ARE talking about family, you know, even if it's extended family. Nobody will want to believe this, even if they want to believe me. Does that make sense?

Anyway, I don't know about these next miles of the journey. I'm making progress, but I'm at the assignment where I'm supposed to ask my Mama about her childhood, you know, get to know my "9-year-old Mama" (rolls eyes). Then, if the trust and rapport are there, share what happened with her. I dunno, maybe I've needed a safe outlet all these years, but I don't know if my Mama, 9-years-old or 65-years-old, is the one. TBH you've been the perfect sounding board in all of this mess.

Ugh! I could just roll over in a fetal position and die right now. This little childhood exercise Jamilah wants me to do is gonna be crazy nerve-racking, and I'll tell you why — because Mamas always know. My Mama is gonna know something's up.

I can feel it.

-M

Chapter 30

On Thu, Jun 1, 2006 at 1:32 PM Krystal Ashe wrote:

Hey, Mikki!

Girl, this is so exciting! Look at you and your progress! Listen, I understand your nervousness and being afraid to talk to your Mom. The fear is valid, but there could be a tremendous light at the end of the tunnel, sis. Why?

Because the phase of the journey you're about to enter — girl, this is where you'll hear the clink-clank of chains rattling and falling to the ground. Just ahead, your tomb doors will open and you'll come out hopping and shedding those grave clothes that were — hear me good — pre-soaked in SECRETS.

Listen... Exposure exterminates secrets!

See, I believe one of the main reasons why healing from past trauma is so hard is because secrets are cancerous shackles that hold you to a life sentence in solitary confinement. And while you're isolated in pain, they convince you that there is no cure, no healing, no freedom in your near or distant future. Secrets can embed themselves in our souls and grow as fast as black mold. You get what I'm saying?

But, you've decided not to take this lying down anymore, Mikki. Now your secrets are about to be defeated.

Think of it this way. You already started your march toward the battlefield when you reached out to me {Clink}. Then, Jamilah {Clank}. Now, your Mom {Clink, Clank}?

Honey, your secrets are nervously clanking around like 'Who does she think she is?' Their stronghold over your life, personality, decisions, happiness, joy, relationships — oh, the handwriting is on the wall, it's all coming to an end.

Go ahead and tell it, Mikki! You'll be surprised by what you might learn about and from your Mom. I'll be right here, praying for grace and peace over you and your mother.

You got this!

Krystal

Chapter 31

On Fri, Jun 2, 2006 at 11:25 PM Mikki Jones wrote:

I appreciate the encouragement, Krystal, and I see what you're saying about how dangerous secrets are. Clearly, the clink-clank of my secret was beginning to damage my hearing. I couldn't hear anyone when they said words like, 'I love you', 'It's going to be okay', 'You can do this', or 'God will heal you'.

While I'm grateful for your cheers, I've got a burning question.

How in the world did you first approach your parents about the white boys?

I mean, I know they know because of the first book, right? But, what did that initial, hard conversation look like?

I'm going to try this convo with Mama within the next few weeks. Any perspective you can give me would be great.

Because even if I really have nothing to fear — girl, I'm scared.

-M

Chapter 32

On Mon, Jun 5, 2006 at 3:12 PM Krystal Ashe wrote:

Hmmmm.... "How" is always a fair question, Mikki — and one of the hardest to answer.

Not because you don't remember "how", but because you want the answer to be meaningful and actionable for the listener. I'll do my best.

First, I want to remind you where I was mentally on my healing journey since all trauma is different.

Healing from family trauma may look different than healing from trauma caused by complete strangers — folks you'll probably never see again. It's not harder or easier — no judgment either way. It's just... different. And, God knows — all parent-child relationships are different, too.

You remember the backstory from *Like It Never Happened*, right? I had lived my life in total competition with white men, always trying to one-up them, whether in class as a kid or in corporate America before I became a full-time author and speaker.

Every bitter blow I was able to land on a white guy was my way of fighting back and retaliating against those white boys since I couldn't fight back at 5. I was a walking, one-woman Black Op (no pun lol) determined to reign pain and suffering on as many white guys as I could.

That was, until God whispered, *"It's time for you to heal"* in my half bath story I told you about in January.

I said all that to say, in my sessions with Jamilah, I eventually discovered just how void I was of the basic human need for — of all things — safety.

I always sensed danger where there wasn't any. Someone was always lurking in the proverbial "bushes" — literally or figuratively — trying to get me, especially when white males were around.

Now, I wouldn't say it was my idea. I was as scared to share my story as you are, and would have loved to remain silent and gone on with life after healing. But my "decision" to share the trauma with my mother stemmed from an understanding of how I had neglected to take advantage of the safe place she represented all those years in my broken life.

My mom loved me and would be mad as hell at those white boys right along with me. She would believe me and be on my side. That's all I wanted. I wanted to be loved and protected. I wanted to be understood and told that they were wrong and it wasn't my fault.

So, Jamilah convinced me to free myself from mental solitary confinement and exterminate the secret.

Mikki, with all of your fear, sis, you're much braver than me. Even though you're scared, you're still willing to have that 1-on-1 convo with your Mom.

Let me tell you how scared I was... I wasn't able to have that conversation with my mother, couldn't do it.

Girl, I wrote her a letter LOL!

Yep. After getting that far along in counseling, after getting most of my voice back and putting sentences together again — there was no way my verbal abilities would have been able to make it through a personal chat about what happened.

So, I did the best I could with what I had. I poured every detail into a "Dear Mom" letter. I told her about that "fat, ghetto babysitter" (what I called her at that time) who did nothing all day but eat Oreos and watch the 'stories'. I told her where it happened — at those Mercy Drive apartments in Orlando, something "Cove". I also described the white boys down to their 70's Shaun Cassidy haircuts. I totally spilled my guts on those sheets of notebook paper, told her how important this letter was to me, and asked her to read it later.

It was hard, but a safer exercise for me versus a 1-on-1. I'd gotten accustomed to writing thoughts and feelings down from my own Forgiveness Diet months earlier. It was a natural progression, I guess.

Krystal

Chapter 33

On Tue, Jun 6, 2006 at 9:57 PM Mikki Jones wrote:

What?!? Man, c'mon, Krystal. A letter!? No you didn't — that's cheating LOL! Jk, sis!

No, I totally understand. And I like what you said — you did the best you could with what you had. See, that's what I love about you, Krystal. You shoot from a "no judgment" zone. That's why so many of your readers can relate to you. It's why I feel so comfortable talking to you.

So, real quick... Girl, what in the world happened? Did you mail the letter to your Mom or just hand it to her? How did your Mom react to what you shared?

If all of that is too personal, please accept my apology. It's just that on one hand, I'm ready to get this conversation thing over with. On the other hand, I have no idea what I'm getting myself into.

But, I'm ready to go, go, go... be done with it. I don't think these fibroids can take much more suspense and pressure.

–M

Chapter 34

On Wed, Jun 21, 2006 at 8:17 AM Mikki Jones wrote:

Good morning, Krystal!

Just checking back in with you, sis. Hope my last question didn't offend you, or come off too pushy about what happened between you and your mom.

You good? Everything OK?

–M

VI

The Womb Was Created to Create

What's that in your belly, sis? Peace or chaos?
Ehh, either way — you're about to burst!
Your due date is almost here.
What's in you will come out of you.

Push!

Chapter 35

On Mon, Jul 3, 2006 at 12:36 PM Krystal Ashe wrote:

Hey Mikki,

How are you, girl? So sorry to go ghost on you like that. I appreciate your patience, sis. I do have some exciting news, though... Long email alert!

A few weeks ago, I received an invitation to be a last-minute panelist and guest lecturer at a conference on the health effects of ACEs, Adverse Childhood Experiences, in San Jose, CA. One of their original invitees had a conflict, and they reached out to me to represent the faith community, share my story, and my road to overcoming an ACEs score of 4. I won't go into all the details here, but you can check out what ACEs scores are and the research <u>here</u> if you'd like to learn more.

I believe the research on ACEs will go even further in the future. You already know that research on how unresolved childhood trauma affects the gynecological health of women, especially women of color, is a heavy focus of mine after years of battling fibroids.

You would've enjoyed the conference, too, Mikki — lots of good information on how important our healing journeys are. Sis, you're not just on this journey to "get over it"; you're changing your cells. You're actually rewiring your brain to have a better quality of life.

So, anyway, I'm glad to be back home — just got back yesterday. Now, where were WE, lordt?? So...listen.

While I was in Cali, I had a chance to talk to my mom one night. Girl, she was so proud to hear that I was speaking at the conference. I don't know how but some kinda way I found the perfect segue to ask my mom the question you asked me last month.

That's right, sis. I didn't quite have an answer for you. Mom and I had never really talked about my letter after I left it with her.

She continued to support my healing process, I'd moved on through my sessions with Jamilah, eventually learned how to maintain my freedom from the pain, wrote a book... Mom's initial reaction was something that just never came up.

And, right in my hotel room that night, I would find out why.

I said, "Ma, you remember that letter I gave you when I was in therapy for my childhood stuff... we never talked about it again. I know it's been years, but... As a parent, what were your thoughts and feelings about what I shared?"

I wasn't ready for her answer.

After reading my letter, Mom said, "I ripped it up and threw it in the garbage."

To be very honest with you, Mikki, I was shocked when she told me this. Almost hurt. Well, let me be real — I was hurt. While I expected Mom to express her anger against those white boys with me, she proceeded to tell me how my letter made her feel like I was blaming her for the incident. Like I was saying if she had been there or if she had been a better mother, I would've never been snatched by those white boys. More words followed about the hardships she was enduring at the time as a single mother — things a 5-year-old me never knew and would've never known.

The conversation was tough, Mikki, real talk. I could feel that little girl rising up in me. She wanted the pain poured into that letter to be about HER experience - not anyone else's. So, to rip up the letter and throw it in the garbage felt like my pain and my experience were discarded like trash, regarded as worthless.

But, here's where healing from victimhood shows up the strongest. You don't discount your pain, but once your pain isn't the complete and total focus of your life, you're able to empathize and have compassion for others' very real thoughts and feelings — even if it's not what you expected.

While I didn't blame my Mom for what happened to me in the letter, she felt that. And I had to get out of my feelings and empathize with how the letter made her feel.

That's also partly why writing this email to you is a little hard...

I know how gung-ho I came off that you were going to share your trauma with your own mother. I know how hard I championed that "exposure exterminates secrets."

Truth is, yes, there are ultimate rewards to getting free from past pain by exposing secrets, but we can't always anticipate how the receivers of our secrets will react.

So, I want to apologize, Mikki, for my one-sided viewpoint on exposing traumatic secrets. I know I'm here to help and guide *you*, but you have actually taught me this lesson — to be more balanced in my approach with others as they tell their stories and pursue freedom and healing.

To some people close to us, ignorance will always be bliss, and there may be a lack of appreciation for your secrets being told. But, there will also be times where the ignorant bliss of others must not cancel your pursuit of healing. Sometimes ignorant bliss is the collateral damage of the pursuit of freedom. Even in these cases, though, I honestly still err on the side of freedom and exposure because they lead to one's healing.

Ignorance doesn't have to be the only road to bliss. Though the truth was hard to swallow, my mom is blissfully proud that I have healed and that my work helps others to heal as well.

Krystal

Chapter 36

On Wed, Jul 5, 2006 at 11:11 PM Mikki Jones wrote:

Krystal!

It's over.

I did it yesterday.

I tried to wait for your email, but Mama came over to see me and I was all sensitive and stuff. I had planned a quiet 4th of July, didn't really feel like mingling with other people — plus my abdomen was a little bloated and achy. I told hubby and the kids to go on over to our friends' house, and just be sure to bring me back some BBQ. Sidebar: Yeah, Jamilah's gonna get me for eating meat. She's been riding me on the mental AND dietary causes of fibroids. But a sista can't barbecue no lettuce, so there's that . Anyhoo...

Girl, I decided to just go for it. Like I was saying... Mama was already starting to ask a bunch of questions. I just broke. Here's how it all went down...

We were sitting on the sofa watching a Law & Order: Special Victims Unit re-run. Sis, Mama stared straight at the TV, wouldn't even glance in my direction when she said, "So what's going on, Mikki? You alright?"

I wanted to scream, "Hell no!", but I would've got popped in my 35-year-old mouth for being *flip*. Instead, I kinda looked at her out of the corner of my eye and responded, "Well, there's something I need to talk to you about, Ma."

She said, "I know", as she grabbed the remote from the end table and cut the TV off.

Can I tell you the room was swollen with silence? Both of us stared straight ahead for what seemed like an eternity. Then, I shifted my body on the sofa to face her. I couldn't believe what I was about to say after 25+ years — but here we go.

"Ma, you remember back in the day how I would spend the night at..."

"... yeah."

And from there, just like that — I figuratively threw up the words. My experience at the age of 9 spilled out on the cushion between us and ran between the seams. I spared her the gory details of what was actually done to me — I wasn't trying to give my Mama a whole heartache. But, as the things my lips were finally able to say out loud hit her, she sat for long moments in total shock. Every now and again, she'd blurt out...

"So, you mean to tell me..."

"Yeah, Ma."

Another few minutes would pass...

"So, what you're saying is..."

Like any parent would, Mama had a lot of questions. See, she loves puzzles like my Grandma loved puzzles. I could see her mind trying to twist and position the pieces of my story together where they all would make sense. But, it didn't make sense. It didn't make sense to me or to her. None of it made sense. None of it should've ever happened. And yet, there we were, staring at the ugly picture of real-life that emerged from all I had to say.

When it was all over, she held me. I broke down some more. Mama told me how sorry she was that I had to go through this, and how strong I was to carry this painful secret for all these years.

"Dog, Mikki..."

That was Mama's way of cussing without cussing, girl. She could feel me.

Strength is a thing in my family; I come from a long line of strong women, many of which carried their secrets and pain to their grave. Maybe this is why I felt so hopeless when we first connected right here in this inbox — I couldn't do what the strong women in my bloodline could do. I couldn't fake it till I made it. I'd tried that and the weight of it all was too much for me.

I'm not saying that Mama or anybody told me to grin and bear it — no one knew what I was going through as a kid. No one. I am saying that as black women, we're taught the unspoken and unwritten rules that instruct us to tattoo that "S" on our chests and never let "them" see Superwoman sweat. Six or seven months ago before you surfaced, not only was I sweating, but I was snot crying, lashing out, and my cape was torn from the top to the bottom. I couldn't put me back together again — not as together as I pretended to be. Lord knows I tried.

Needless to say, Krystal, this was a breakthrough. And, though it was hard and I was so nervous at first, I'm actually glad I had this talk with my Mama.

I hear the journey was a little different between you and your Mom, but as you said — all parent-child relationships are different. I'm still so glad that you shared that experience with me, no worries at all. I knew something must've been up when I didn't hear back from you quickly.

I'm glad this particular stress is over for me.

Now, let me sign-off and get ready for my OB/GYN appointment in the morning. Them darn fibroids just won't quit.

-M

Chapter 37

On Thu, Jul 6, 2006 at 8:47 AM Krystal Ashe wrote:

Wow, Mikki. You did it! Myyyy girl!

Sis, I can't find the words to type how proud I am of you, and how happy I am that you had such a supportive experience. I know you are sooo glad all that fear and worry can now be put to rest. I hope this experience fuels your strength and courage, Mikki. Knowing that if you can survive some of your scariest moments on this journey, who says you can't reach that finish line and thrive!

You have an amazing Mom. We both do; it's not easy to receive and process the information we have shared about our personal trauma. Mothers are still human, though like you said, sometimes we think they're Superwoman.

And you know what else, we are very blessed to have mothers with who we could even envision sharing our pain. There are many women out there whose mothers may not be in a frame of mind, for whatever reason — or even alive to help their adult daughters process ugly secrets from their childhood.

So, yeah, shout out to all the moms out there, like ours, for being that rock and safe place that their daughters never knew they would ever need.

Sorry to hear about the fibroids, good grief, flaring up again? Are you having a full ultrasound or just an annual PAP?

-Krystal

Chapter 38

On Sat, Jul 8, 2006 at 10:26 AM Mikki Jones wrote:

Hey Krystal,

So, I'm probably going to be a little MIA for a sec. I dunno. It just all depends on how things turn out.

I went to the doctor. Yes, I had an ultrasound, PAP, and more — a whole lot of probing, sticking, and scraping that us women with these doggone gyno issues could really do without.

Yep, the fibroids are still there and growing, all 12 of them, but they're still the size of small lemons on down to those large bullet grapes you see at the grocery store. The cysts are there, too, but they told me that they could come and go depending on my cycle, stress levels, etc. Cool.

I kind of expected all of that news, but there was something my doctor found that caught me and her off guard — and, no, I'm not pregnant, thank you sweet baby Jesus!

We can manage fibroids and cysts, that's not the problem. But, sis, when the doctor says the "p" word — polyps — that's when it's time to spring into action and play zero games. Since they are precursors to cancer, you never know when those things have had enough and they start transforming into real trouble.

I have 2 in my uterus that need to be removed asap. They'll do a biopsy to detect whether there are any cancerous cells and we'll go from there.

To keep it real — I'm honestly annoyed, Krystal. It just seems like every 3 steps forward, I'm knocked 5 steps back. Surgery, and all that comes with it, Lord. I just had enough on my plate making the decision to try to heal this year emotionally and mentally. Now I gotta deal with the physical? After-surgery pain, bed rest — with my busy schedule?

This is some bull. Sigh.

I go under next Friday, 7/14. I took a week off from my job to heal up.

Please say a prayer for your girl.

-M

Chapter 39

On Mon, Jul 10, 2006 at 6:17 AM Krystal Ashe wrote:

Wow. Ok, Mikki. You got it, sis! Prayers up high!

I can imagine you weren't expecting that kind of news from a general diagnostic visit — neither was I. But the good thing is they caught those polyps early. And you are 100% correct. When those things show up, you don't play around, you don't lollygag on getting them removed. You act fast! Good for you, Mikki!

Have you told Jamilah yet? Which reminds me... how far have you gotten with her tie-in of mental health and gynecological issues? I know she's going to have some insight to share.

Thinking back to when I was in therapy under her care and practically living in my gynecologist's office, I had no clue that the childhood trauma I was dealing with likely had a major negative impact on my physical health — specifically in my uterus. See, back in the day while I was still corporate, I was a songwriter in my spare time. My thing was setting words to music that moved the heart. Girl, been a creative all my life, I guess.

Jamilah's whole mantra was how fertile and creative the black woman is and, since our wombs are our creative center, we either create beauty or chaos within them - no middle ground. We were going to *create* one way or the other — the "what" we create was not only up to us, but heavily influenced by our experiences, environments, and how we deal with them.

Girl, did she ever show or tell you about the pictures of fibroids removed that had teeth and hair in them? I think they call them teratomas.

Sis, I don't know about you, but those pictures freaked me out back then. It was like the womb — all by itself — created these little monsters that used the blood supply of the uterus as a life source.

If I remember how passionate Jamilah was, I know she still believes that the prevalence of fibroids in black women - 2 out of 3 experiencing complications from fibroids in their lifetime - weighs heavily on the state of our minds and spirits.

Have you ever noticed how so many successful, driven, BOSS black women have fibroids or some other kind of gynecological issue? I was amazed. I'd have random conversations with other successful women, and they would admit, "Yeah sis, I have fibroids, too." It became so commonplace, so often that conversations ultimately shifted from "Do you have fibroids?" to "How many fibroids are *you* fighting, sis?"

See, this was another reason why writing *Like it Never Happened* was so important to me. While I was dealing with the white boys, other women were dealing with uncles, fathers, cousins, boyfriends, random guy at the party — all of these painful memories locked in a dark, secret place inside our wombs.

The womb keeps score, Mikki. We don't naturally consider the fact that whatever is buried alive will eventually claw its way to the surface.

And, because hiding our pain was such an unspoken, unwritten rule of engagement, we privately ravaged the rotten fruit of past trauma and swallowed the seeds whole. This was the black woman's normal — bury the pain, dress up in success, super-glue the got-it-going-on mask, and parade around in our BOSS-ness like nothing ever happened. Sure, everything's fine.

This is no indictment, Mikki, I get us. Sometimes faking "fine" seems so much easier than doing the real work to heal.

And it is. I think we both have a lifetime of receipts to show just how much effort and commitment it takes to heal your soul.

But, the hard work it takes to heal will never compare to the liberating rewards of being free.

Mikki, think of your surgery as "Clean up on aisle one!" It's hard work, it's a chore — but it's cleaning out the damage and abnormalities in your womb so you can create what is beautiful, again.

That right there was our intended normal — to create and bring forth beauty and splendor.

So the weekend around your surgery, I'll be on travel again. This time, I'll be in D.C. at the 2006 *Conference on Trauma-Informed Care*. I love how more and more medical conferences invite the voices of non-physicians to share their experience around the impact of trauma on health.

Who knows, Mikki. By the time you reach your finish line, we might be able to travel together and partner to help others heal.

I know you don't feel like you're there yet, and helping someone else is the farthest thing from your mind while you put on YOUR oxygen mask. But honestly, I think about it often. I believe so strongly that you're going to make it, sis. And what a beautiful miracle that will be when it happens.

Sending faith-filled prayers for a successful surgery and swift recovery, sis. Trust that you're constantly in my thoughts, Mikki.

I know this was a long email, but we're going to miss each other for a quick second. Will drop you a line to catch up and hear all the details.

Be encouraged, Mikki... God goes before you, with you, and after you.

-Krystal

Chapter 40

On Thu, Jul 13, 2006 at 10:35 PM Mikki Jones wrote:

Hey Krystal,

I imagine you're packing and getting ready for your trip. Have a great time, sis! I'm just sitting here at my desk, thinking... and hungry. You know how you always get hungry the night before surgery when the doctors tell you that you can't eat past a certain time. Girl, I wouldn't even be thinking about food if I weren't under doctor's orders lol!

So, I had a session with Jamilah yesterday. I wanted to squeeze in one more visit before I'm on bed rest, keep my head in the right space. Yeah girl, you already know. We talked A LOT about womb health and the causes of dysfunction in our creative space.

I could only think about my years of destructive thinking and how these thoughts had festered and affected my reproductive health. It's crazy how negative thoughts and unresolved pain can take deep root, and the fruit of that thought can manifest into a fibroid months — even years — later! I can see why Jamilah's so adamant for women to move swiftly to get help after traumatic events — she's trying to help us ward off long-term physical, mental, and emotional effects of this stuff that won't show up till later.

I remember back in January thinking I wasn't ready to heal, or maybe I couldn't handle what it would take to a) face or b) heal from all my stuff.

While I'm still working hard and got more hills to climb, yesterday's session made me even more grateful that I started when I did. Who knows what future *infectious growths* I'm blocking right now because I decided to *stop the pain from leaking and drowning my divine purpose* — that's how Jamilah put it, I liked that.

It was after she spoke those words that I opened up to her about my miracle birth. Did I ever share that story with you?

Sis, me and fibroids go wayyyy back, unfortunately. Back to before I was even born. Heck, if fibroids had had their way, I would've never been born.

See, my mom was filled with fibroids at the same time she was carrying me. So much so that even at her 3rd, 5th, 9th month — the doctors *never* heard my heartbeat. Girl, can you imagine that? Mom's fibroids were so massive that they smothered the sound of my heart.

Little did anyone know that, as a developing fetus, I was in there fighting with fibroid tumors for the blood supply of my mother. Me *and* the fibroids were growing.

So, early in the pregnancy, Mom was convinced — "I'm carrying around a dead fetus in my stomach." She thought I was either a dead baby swallowed up by the tumors, or a deformed, under-produced fetus. Either way, I would've come to the same conclusion.

While my mom was on the east coast dealing with the pregnancy, my dad was in California working one day — and the strangest thing happened.

He was a painter, and on the ladder in mid-stroke with his paintbrush, he had a vision that my mom had made plans for an abortion.

(Mind you, she had made plans to abort me, but she never told him. Never told anybody. It was early enough to do so; she saw no use in carrying a dead fetus to full term.)

Girl, my dad leaped off that ladder, ran to the phone, and called my mom. What he said when she answered the phone changed the course of my entire life forever —

"*We don't kill no babies. God is able...*"

He went on to tell mom how the Holy Spirit showed him in a vision that plans were being made to abort me. I can imagine how shocked my mom was to receive that call from the other side of the country — especially when she hadn't told anyone but the doctor. It was a sign she ultimately couldn't ignore.

Mom agreed to carry the pregnancy to full-term.

The Thursday afternoon of my birth, doctors removed mass after mass of fibroid tumors from my mom via C-section. With all the tumors removed, what did they find buried in the back?

Me. A healthy, breathing baby girl with a strong heartbeat!

Mom says she remembered hearing when the whole operating room gasped — it was a miracle. While doctors thought they were going in to remove a stillborn baby, God had different plans. My newborn cry was the roar of victory that let them all know — nothing can kill what God wants to live.

Wow.

It's funny. Before, I wouldn't even think about my birth story. I was too busy being mad at God. I thought it was so unfair for Him to miraculously bring me through all of that birth drama to be born for childhood trauma that would linger through adulthood. Feel me? Who does that?

But between you, Jamilah, family, God — I'm starting to re-member my purpose, put my reason for still being here back in proper perspective. As Jamilah says, *God's original intent for me.* I guess there's no way God fights that hard for a baby with no purpose.

It all gives deeper meaning to Jeremiah 1:5 for me, *"Before I formed you in your mother's womb, I knew you..."*

Girl, let me take my behind to bed and stop my mind from racing. I've gotta be at the hospital by 6:30 AM for check-in.

I'm feeling encouraged and ready to get this chapter over with. The prayers are working, sis, pls keep sending. And if I haven't said it before, thank you for letting me borrow some of your strength these past six months. I promise somehow to give it back.

I appreciate you, Krystal.

TTYL

-M

Chapter 41

On Fri, Jul 14, 2006 at 8:07 PM Mikki Jones wrote:

hey sis i survivd. thx God..

M

Chapter 42

On Sat, Jul 15, 2006 at 11:12 PM Krystal Ashe wrote:

Hey there, Mikki!

Yay! Girl, of course you survived! To God be the glory!

Now, I only have one question — who let you sneak and send me that crazy email LOL! You're supposed to be resting :).

I was so tickled, sis; I could picture you coming back from the anesthesia, looking for your cell, hiding the phone under the cover, trying to type fast... too funny!

I'm so glad things went well, Mikki. Now it's time to continue your physical healing by doing exactly what the doctors tell you to do. Please do right, sis! This is important for you, mentally and emotionally, too.

In the meantime, guess what? I have a little something for you :).

I was scrolling through folders on my laptop here in the hotel the other night (BTW, this Conference on Trauma-Informed Care has been ahhhhmazing, deets later!), and I ran across my old "Krystal's Music" folder. I don't know why now; hadn't clicked around in there for years, girl. But it pretty much turned into a late-night memory lane of songs I wrote back in the day — or left unwritten.

Anyway, there was this one song file that stuck out to me. It was at the bottom of the list, the only one still named "Untitled.mp3".

I clicked the small triangle to press play. It had a strong Middle Eastern pan flute lead, and in the background, you can hear the harp and the shaker dancing in the cool rain — all to my randomly spoken syllables — no real words.

It took me less than 5 seconds to remember what I was actually listening to.

Remember, years ago during my healing journey, like you, I had no words. And the few words I did find, I sure couldn't say them out loud. I couldn't say out loud what those boys had done to me, how it jacked up my life, but I wanted so desperately to have a way to talk to God about it — without actually talking to God about it if that makes any sense.

So, I turned to music.

Music was a healing balm for me, Mikki — physically, mentally, and emotionally. And, no one could create music that expressed the way I was feeling, except me.

There's a secret SOS signal transmitted throughout the 2 minutes of *Untitled.* It was in actuality *a prayer.*

Sis, the song was my way of secretly telling God (or sometimes just saying out loud) what had happened and how I desperately needed help — without saying one single "word". The shame and desperation were all secretly encoded throughout every note, every instrument in this song, and no one would ever know. No one but God would hear what I was saying that I couldn't say to anyone else. He would feel the emotion, feel my pain, hear my hidden cry for help, and one day rescue me and take me *across* my finish line to freedom.

And, God did just that, Mikki!

Hearing this song again brought tears to my eyes for the woman singing it. I cried for her pain, for her inability to find her words or a safe place for them when she did. But, I also cried out to God in worship. The Almighty I AM had broken me out of my prison where the devil had pronounced a life sentence of bondage in those bushes — over me and my purpose.

Sis, I truly believe that a Godly prayer chain is one where you pass on your answered prayers to someone else who's waiting for the exact same answer.

Mikki, this prayer song is now yours (see attached).

Listen to it while you're recovering, during your prayer time, when you're feeling low, when you're angry and frustrated, during worship — whenever you want to tell God how you're feeling and the words refuse to come. Go ahead, make every syllable your own.

This song is no longer listed in my folder as "Untitled" — I now call it *Mikki's Prayer.*

Love you, sis! Get well soon...

Krystal

1 Attachments
Mikkis-Prayer.mp3

Chapter 43

On Tue, Jul 20, 2006 at 12:21 PM Mikki Jones wrote:

Hey Krystal,

Girl, I finally found a moment to breathe — without much post-surgery pain. Grateful. Between the soreness in my abdomen and the soreness in my throat from the breathing tube, let's just say it feels exactly like I've been run over by a Mack truck.

The doctor called yesterday to say that the biopsy came back negative for any cancer. Glory! So while I can't jump up and down for the next 6-8 weeks, I'm definitely in bed with my laptop waving my hands, and wigglin' the heck out of these toes LOL!

Wow. How nice of you, sis. *Mikki's Prayer.* Has a nice ring to it!

When I saw the attachment, I couldn't wait to plug in my headphones and press play. The song grabbed my soul at the first note. And then, I pressed play over and over and over and over again. I really can't get enough of *Mikki's Prayer,* sis. MY very own prayer :).

And I could hear it, too, Krystal. I could hear the private conversation with God happening just beneath the music. Every syllable echoed what my voice couldn't say out loud in plain English. And now? On that "Ohhhhhhh dahhhhhh…" part? Girl, I can't help it. My hand lifts in surrender and worship to God involuntarily. I feel gracefully disarmed and totally dependent on His valiant rescue at that part.

I feel my soul healing every time I play it, Krystal. And, if my soul is healing, then my physical, mental, and emotional healing is happening, too. I remember those two-ton boulders on my soul you talked about in January. They're getting lighter. I can feel a slight shift after months of therapy with our beloved Jamilah. Funny, that sounds just like her, doesn't it? *Beloved…*

I really miss seeing Jamilah. Girl, you know she's already emailed me her plant-based, anti-inflammatory foods list to help me recover LOL. Now, if only she could send me an anti-inflammatory recipe to ward off family drama.

You guessed it. I've had some family check up on me, you know — a phone call here, a text there. Word kinda gets around when your mother sends out a "keep Mikki in your prayers" group text. Lord. Folks come out the woodworks. I even heard from my uncle. He's sick himself, on regular dialysis, but he called me talking 'bout, "So. I heard. You ain't no spring chicken no more, Mikki!" His wife was in the background cackling; I dunno why she was laughing so hard. She's got years on me. Unc is my father figure… he has been since my dad passed when I was a teen. I really miss him.

Other family members call and they want to get all in your business. Girl, my cousin wanted to know the exact name of the surgery so she could go and Google it. Everybody's an Internet doctor these days. But, I'm still not comfortable having people in my business like that. I'm probably just as guarded as the next woman who's had any kind of gynecological surgery.

I know one thing. I can't wait to get back on my feet and graduate from these sponge baths to soaking in a tub surrounded by candles again. Looks like I'm back on another journey in search of normalcy. Welp. At least this time, I have my own prayer song to carry me through.

Anyway, I feel like I'm rambling. Must be these Tylenol3's, girl. I think it's time for an afternoon nap.

Will be in touch over the next few weeks as I get back on my feet and back to work. It's crazy how life happens and you have to shift gears for a second, you know, slow things down. But don't worry, I've come too far with my childhood stuff to go back to January. Gee, thanks alot LOL! JK!

Hope you are well, Krystal.

Till soon,

M

Chapter 44

On Sat, Jul 22, 2006 at 9:11 AM Krystal Ashe wrote:

Sounds good, Mikki! So glad you're enjoying your prayer song, and I'm overjoyed to hear that you're making progress — on ALL fronts!

In a few months, I'll be traveling to Florence to attend a *Reducing Revictimization Symposium* sponsored by UNICEF-Innocenti Research Center, and then I'll be participating in their *Study of Public Policy and Violence Against Children* through October. Girl, God keeps me on my toes with some great learning opportunities. Looking forward to spreading my wings internationally for a second; was getting a little cabin fever here in Houston.

You take as much time as you need to heal up, sis. Stay gentle and patient with yourself. We all heal at our own pace.

Continued prayers,
Krystal

Chapter 45

On Fri, Aug 25, 2006 at 8:25 AM Mikki Jones wrote:

Hey Krystal,

How you, sis? Hope you're enjoying Italy. Your travel engagements are getting sexier and sexier, girl LOL! I promise every time I hear of your travels, I wish I could be there — showing up all healed and whole like you do, ready to take on the evils of trauma that others are facing.

Instead? I'm still here, sis, coming on down the stretch of this bed rest LOL!

So recently, I got crazy bored and I went thumbing through the pages of *Like it Never Happened* again — for like the umpteenth time. (BTW, I'm still trying to graduate to your 2nd book, *Renouncing Victimhood*, but I'm not quite there yet.)

And do you know what hit me?

I was thinking here I have a pretty close relationship with one of my fave authors, ever, and I still have some burning, unanswered questions about her book. So if you don't mind, sis, please direct your attention to Chapter 8 LOL!

But seriously, all jokes aside, Krystal. I have always wondered about that encounter you had in the 2nd grade. The one where you kissed that little white boy at the playground, remember? You wrote:

> *"What diabolical joy it gave me to hear little Patrick O'Reilly squeal like a pig headed for the slaughterhouse, tears welling up in his eyes, face flush red..."*

Now, when I first read the story, I was thinking, "If y'all don't come get this little black girl and tell her to get her act together. Leave that little white boy alone before they come get you!"

Girl, something seemed to snap. What really happened with you right there? How, or better yet, *why* in the world did that happen, you know, after what those boys did to you in Kindergarten? Many readers would probably think you'd stay far away from white boys as possible after that...

Just always wondered.

M

Chapter 46

On Fri, Sep 1, 2006 at 7:42 AM Krystal Ashe wrote:

Hey, Mikki!

Hope all is well, sis! I trust your physical healing process went well, and you're back in the swing of things. Thanks for your patience! Yes, girl, Florence is beautiful!

So, good ol' Chapter 8, huh? Lordy. Only for you, Mikki LOL!

Wow. I must say I was so embarrassed by that story, but it's the God-honest truth. We were in P.E. on the playground, a bunch of wilding 2nd graders running around playing the kissing game and who had the "cooties". What in the world made me target little Patrick? It was probably the fear in his eyes when we saw each other across the playground, like, *"Ohhhh no, this black girl is gonna give me her cooties!"* Being the "cute boy" in the class probably didn't help him either. He took off climbing up the monkey bars; I took off in hot pursuit. Me and some other little girls pulled him down, but I was the one who kissed his red-flushed cheek, while he yelled in pretentious, dying agony.

Though it was just kids fooling around at recess, unbeknownst to that little Irish boy — he was catching all of my 7-year-old wrath. In hindsight, I was so mean and cruel because I believe, as a mature adult now, that he was terrified — whether we were all giggling and he was play yelling or not.

"...diabolical joy?" Yep. That was my adult assessment of what my 7-year-old self was feeling when I wrote LINH. All she could see in his contorted face was the disgust *she* felt to have someone's nasty hands covering her mouth — heck, that was the real cooties. All I could see in his petrified eyes were my terrorized eyes when those white boys grabbed me and pressed that knife against my neck. To this day, without even trying hard, I can still see how the light reflected off of it.

I do wonder, though, if Patrick O'Reilly remembers that day on the playground. I hope that experience didn't damage him in any way. Sis, if I could find him today, I'd sincerely apologize.

This is why I applaud you and anyone else who finds the courage to acknowledge trauma in their life and seeks help. *Hurt people hurt people* is not just a cliche. Unhealed trauma is the devil's playground, and he's controlling how fast the iron carousel spins and how high you go on those swings.

This is also why I couldn't just move on with my peachy, healed life, and not reach back and help someone else. Now, I can't send all these emails to everyone who sends me a random SOS, but you were the first to be so bold and risky, so unconventional, Mikki — which meant you were either on your last leg or serious about getting help and doing the work — or both.

If I haven't said it in a minute, Mikki, I'm really proud of you and the work you're putting in. And, I'm glad that God would use my words to help you in whatever small way I can — through email no less, who knew?

Keep going, girl, you are doing the daggone thing!

Krystal

VII

The Finish Line

It doesn't always look, sound, or feel like it.
But, you're at the end.
The end of what? It all depends...

Chapter 47

On Sat, Sep 9, 2006 at 8:25 AM Mikki Jones wrote:

Hey Krystal,

I've got some good news for us!

Yesterday, I completed a milestone that I frankly never would've reached without your support and guidance — it was my 7th month anniversary of counseling sessions with our beloved Jamilah, yay!

I'm so proud of myself, Krystal. I had no clue, but while we were in session (the first one since the surgery), Jamilah was flipping back through my file and noticed the date. I've been doing the work to heal, sis, for seven months now! I've still got some miles to go, but you of all people know how important it is to celebrate big and small victories. Jamilah and I had a great time talking about the early days — how it was hard for me to open up at first... remember how I thought my forgiveness graduation ceremony would kill me LOL and I was so mad at God? Wow.

As I was reading your explanation about the playground story, that all made sense, sis. When you read that story with an adult eye, you can unrealistically expect a child to process pain with an adult perspective. It's just not gonna happen. Children both hurt and process pain with the same under-developed, child-like feelings that are natural to them.

You know... a relevant follow-up question would be — how did you grow in your interactions with white males *after* the playground? In college? In corporate? Girl, I hope things didn't get worse...

Jamilah and I talked about how hurt people hurt themselves, too. That's kinda how you found me — or rather I found you — ready to hurt myself that January night to end the pain permanently. Factor in age and the fact that not all "hurt" is intentional or premeditated, it helped me to understand the playground story even more... and some of my own childhood shenanigans.

I'll tell you an embarrassing secret, Krystal, given you were so open about when you kissed Patrick. You weren't the only one acting out of pain in elementary school. I can't believe I'm about to share this... those invisible email hackers are gonna have a field day with this LOL.

Ok. Let me start by saying, I can't stand to hear adults calling little girls "fast" — especially without spending some time with the little girl to see what's on her mind, where she's been, what she's going through, ya know? I shared this with Jamilah at the end of our session.

See, that's what the lunchroom ladies called *me* in the 5th grade — "Oooooh, she fasssst!", with their turned-up noses and smirky lips.

It was Halloween 1980. The whole school was dressed up in their best Halloween costumes. The student with the most original or funniest costume would win a prize (I forget what the prize was).

Anyway, I had this costume all planned out in my head. Now, I knew my sanctified Mama wasn't going to approve, so I had my friend stash the costume at her house, and I'd come by to pick things up before we went to the bus stop.

I'd taken one of my Mama's wigs from her mannequin heads — check! My girlfriend let me borrow some high-heeled shoes and makeup — check! To this day, I have zero idea where I got the balloons from...

I waited until lunchtime to go to the bathroom and put my costume together. All of the teacher judges would be in the cafeteria, and students would cheer for their favorites as students in the lunch line filed in.

Bam! I was all decked out. It was the moment of truth and time to shine.

When I entered the lunchroom doors, the entire lunchroom of some 90+ students erupted in laughter and finger-pointing! Some of the little boys got out of their seats and ran up to me to grab or touch my "costume". Most of the teacher judges just stared — jaws-dropped in total disbelief.

Sigh. I get it.

They had never in their lives seen a pregnant prostitute clown, decked out with balloons for her breasts and booty! I could barely walk in those high heels, trying to keep the belly cushion in place and struggling to see straight through the wig. But my breasts and booty? I was the funniest, most voluptuous 5th grader in the school.

Jiggling and sashaying my hips, I made it to the serving line, and (like a

137

fool) announced to the lunchroom ladies that I was a pregnant prostitute clown — let's just say that didn't sit very well with those older black "aunties".

"Chiiile, she'll be pregnant by junior high... fasssst self", I heard one lady whisper. Another lady looked at me like she wanted to take her big serving spoon and whoop my behind on sight. All they could do was roll their eyes and shake their heads.

Needless to say, they'd never let a 10-year-old, pregnant prostitute clown win the school's Halloween contest LOL. I was so disappointed. I knew I had won. I thought all the kids loved my costume...

That day still upsets me when I think about it now. My anger vacillates between the lunchroom ladies and the family member who tried to turn me out. But honestly? I can't really blame the lunchroom ladies too too much. Thirty-plus years later and I still have no explanation for my behavior that day other than the mismanaged trauma of a child.

Now, when I told Jamilah this story in session, I honestly laughed and shook my own head at the visual, like, what in the world, Mikki?!

Jamilah, of course, would only smile back politely. She knew this sort of *acting out* was a manifestation of my pain. She took me much deeper. I didn't want to go there.

She began to dissect "why a prostitute"? Why did I think that was acceptable? Why did I need to be seen like that so badly to win the approval of others? What seed had 9-year-old Mikki been exposed to that informed her, within a year, that her value had only grown to the equivalent of a woman who sold her body for sex?

You see that, Krystal? These were questions nobody ever bothered to ask me before they looked down on me.

The truthful answers made me angry. I could see how the attempt to groom me to *please others* ranked me no higher than a mere object. And objects don't feel, they simply comply with whatever sexual favor is asked of them. And little Mikki had failed the test and kept begging for a re-take.

I may have been oblivious at 10, but now I see clearly where the root of being a people-pleaser was reinforced in my life.

M

Chapter 48

On Sun, Sep 17, 2006 at 11:10 AM Krystal Ashe wrote:

Mikki,

I'm not gonna lie to you, girl. That story made me holler at first! Like you said, just the visual alone of you in that wig and balloons flopping around LOL! Whew, chile!

But, after more thought, I feel like one of those cafeteria ladies should've grabbed you, taken you to the front office, and called your parents, like, *"Have you seen your child's Halloween costume?"*

Now, if your Mom is anything like mine, you would've gotten your behind beat down from the school to the parking lot... on the way home... at the red light... AND at the house LOL — especially if that was your Mama's *good* wig!

I know it probably would have crushed your Mom, but, I can't help but wonder what would have been different in your life had *someone* taken the time to check you — AND check *on* you. I totally agree that if someone had asked you the same questions Jamilah did — *before* looking down on you — that may have had a positive impact on young Mikki. They had school counselors available in the '80s, yes?... and no one heard the cry for help in your acting out? Amazing.

So, we're about to get out of here in a few weeks. Girl, Florence owes me nothing, and I feel even more empowered to help young victims of violent crime and trauma.

Speaking of... did you catch this news over in the states last month, how an 18-year-old Austrian woman named Natascha Kampusch was snatched and held for 8 years by her kidnapper — and she finally escaped? It made both national and international headlines; all we could do at the Research Center was rejoice! I'm really praying for her healing journey ahead. You and I both can only imagine the road ahead for Natascha — returning home to family and friends after so much has happened to and with her for the past eight years.

I remember staring at the TV in amazement as I watched the news report. You know what this taught me? That our personal stories of trauma, abuse, violence — you name it — yes, it's all horrible and tragic. But, we cannot let our story convince us that no one else on earth knows what we're going through. You're not the only one, I'm not the only one who's experienced trauma and hardship. The reality is, and it's hard to acknowledge this, but, there's something to be grateful for, even in the jacked-up crap we've been through.

My Mom has this saying, "Things could always be worse." Here I am, my life in all kinds of disarray because I was snatched and got away the same day. And Natascha was over there in Austria — snatched at age 10 AND KEPT against her will for 8 long years.

Don't get me wrong. I'm not beating up on myself, nor am I minimizing the impact of that day in the bushes. But, I am giving myself, and you, Mikki — permission to find a point of gratitude by realizing it could've been worse.

I'll be back stateside next month. I was so ready to run from Houston, and now all I can think about is my own bed, I can't wait!

Hey. I've got an idea. What do you think about us picking a city and finally meeting up face-to-face over the holidays? It'll be crazy fun... a time to celebrate your progress! Let me know!

Till soon,

Krystal

Chapter 49

On Thu, Oct 5, 2006 at 10:10 PM Krystal Ashe wrote:

Hey Mikki,

Girl, I've got this astronomical layover in Frankfurt before I reach American soil (I'm talking 9hrs), thought I'd drop you a line to pass this slow-ticking time.

So, I was scrolling through our recent emails, and I noticed that you asked about white males and how I'm handling interactions with them now. I think I got so caught up in the 1980 Halloween story that I forgot to address that part.

The short story is, God has healed me from all of that drama to the point where I can easily interact with white men without panic attacks, nightmares, etc. Now, though I'm still open to love again after a narcissistic marriage, it'll never happen with a white guy. There are still some boundaries for me. Understand this, white men didn't only represent personal trauma for me, because I grew up hearing how white police officers beat my father in the '60s. So there was a lot to unpack.

The long story is, from the playground to college to corporate America, white men were always my enemy. I had grown to play this imaginary game with them. If it were between them and me, they would never come out on top. There was always a hidden competition. Always an angle for me to win and dominate especially if a white man was in the game.

Funny, I remember my first semester in college. A young black girl from the projects, with a single mother, headed to the University of Florida — the largest university in Florida at the time and a PWI (predominately white institution), of course. I don't know what compelled my pro-black self to attend a PWI vs. an HBCU. I guess when your Mom has already told you, "*I ain't got it*", you go where the scholarship checks are cut.

The class was freshman English 101. Dr. Richards played both English professor and theater director at UF, which meant he loved the written word and had a flair for the dramatic.

In a class full of Brads and Kyles who lived in the best dorms on campus (while I lived in a triple dorm room with two of my besties and no A/C) I wanted to stand out, be a top-performing student amongst this sea of whiteness.

It was our final essay, five double-spaced typed pages on any topic we'd like to write about. This essay had to stand above the crowd. I remember bouncing some ideas off of my uncle. He always had a way with words.

During our final class, Dr. Richards would read his top pick for the semester. He began by describing it as *a stunning essay that embodied the mastery of crafting an introduction, thesis, and supporting claims therein —*

girl, he said something to that effect.

"Take a listen to the first sentence, ladies and gentlemen..." Mikki, the last thing I wanted to hear was somebody's dumb essay about their privileged life. My mind kept drifting off to *The Set* where all the cute boys on campus were hanging out before their next period.

"The mind."

Girl, I jerked my head up so fast, I know my classmates saw me and put two and three together. Hilarious. My My uncle told me that that two-word sentence-no-sentence was a winner, and Dr. Richards sold it as if it were the opening line of a Shakespearean play.

It was the look on all of the Brads' and Kyles' faces for me. I won. I'd beat them again. They were defeated by the best, this black girl from the 'hood, whose government assistance paved the way for them to learn the intricacies of essay writing —from me.

So, no Mikki. It didn't stop at the playground or in college. Being able to walk away from the *one-up a white boy* game didn't end until... I sacrificed my anger, wrath, pride... and picked up enough humility to realize I needed help. That leg of my healing helped birth *Renouncing Victimhood*, but I'm not gonna worry you about my 2nd book — I already know how you feel about it LOL. That book goes against all kinds of social norms that keep victims justifiably victimized. It'll be here when you're ready.

Girl, have you ever realized that Jamilah has a whole counseling practice helping women heal from trauma on a day-to-day basis? It must wear on her at times. There's pain being suffered, managed, dealt with all around us. Sis, I can't imagine the stories of her other clients — because our stories alone, just you and I, are enough to make anybody tired.

Grateful that God chose and equipped her to do her work, aren't you?

Well, let me take this quick nap before my connecting flight... not like I need to sleep before an 11-hour flight, but my eyes are heavy and my internal clock is off...

K

Chapter 50

Hey Krystal,

Welcome back home, sis! I can imagine your days right now are filled with some good sleep, trying to get your body back on central standard time. I hope you're doing well and catching up on life back here in the states.

Wow! Girl, that college story. Sounds like you really had it bad for white guys. And, I don't blame you one bit, no judgment. Krystal, you're like this living, walking, breathing testimony of how *healing happens*, as Jamilah always says. It's great to have a close example of what's possible, see healing up close and personal through the eye (or words) of someone who has done the work and reached the finish line.

You'll be pleased to know that I've accelerated my therapy schedule, added an additional session with Jamillah per month to really begin to wrap things up. It's been grueling, taking up a lot of my time and energy, but she says I'm making tremendous progress and I'm really 'bout to turn the corner. There are just a couple of things I need to release and let go of, some things that are under my complete control. I just have to make the decision and stick to it, she said.

You can probably relate to this, Krystal, having had to let the white boys go. It was a pain that you knew, the white boy game was a familiar part of your life. It's hard to let those things go that have been a part of you for so long. It forces you to answer the questions, "*Who am I if I don't have _____ to be depressed about? How can I justify my limp some days, and walk straight other days without my _____ crutch?*"

I have to say, Jamilah is after every crutch in my life right now. I don't think I'll be able to hold her at bay much longer LOL!

While leaving the last session, I told her that there's a *slight* possibility that you and I might meet up in person over the holidays, or at least before the year is out. Girl, that made Jamilah cheer and give me a big hug. She got all excited (not sure why), and kept saying, "*The sooner the better. The sooner the better.*" She said this would be a great segway to our next few sessions, and she'd tell me more then. Cool, I guess.

Ok, so do you eat meat? Pescatarian? I'm already thinking in my mind where we could go during our long, overdue meetup! It's amazing how I started this journey with you long before our emails, watching you speak at that Ted Talk. To go from being hesitant to approach you — to now getting your invitation to connect 1:1? Man. Life is so funny, Krystal. I could only imagine this blessing...

Will touch base again soon! I'm super excited, too!

Mikki

Chapter 51

On Thu, Oct 12, 2006 at 5:57 PM Krystal Ashe wrote:

Hey Mikki,

Aww, that is so sweet of Jamilah, she's such an amazing woman. Girl, she's probably just thrilled to see her clients come together in unified healing and wholeness. I can promise you that she's probably seen pieces of me in you, and vice versa. How long has she been hearing about our long-distance email relationship? I'm so honored that I could embody and champion Jamilah's mantra, *healing happens*, for you, sis. She's drilled those words into all of us, I'm sure. Keep doing that hard work, you're closer than you think.

I'm checking my calendar for a few dates later this month or early November, cool? You're welcome to come here to Houston (where there's only one Turkey Leg Hut LOL), or I can fly out to Atlanta for a fun weekend, your choice .

Standing by...

Krystal

Chapter 52

On Fri, Oct 27, 2006 at 1:23 AM Mikki Jones wrote:

Krystal,

So, sis, you've probably gathered that this month doesn't work well for me. Thanks for your patience, but... we may have to put off our meet-up for a while.

My last session with Jamilah was pretty interesting, to say the least. I thought the accelerated work was a good idea, we both did. I thought, "The sooner the better" was a good thing. But she's coming hard for my stuff, challenging me in different ways than I've experienced before and it's extremely stressful and uncomfortable.

Actually. You know what? Maybe we should put off meeting up, indefinitely. We've really had such a great connection over email this past year, well, almost a year. And, email is so much easier on time and budgets, wouldn't you agree?

In the meantime, please keep me in prayer, Krystal. For real.

I heard from my uncle and his wife, again. So, apparently, they'll be in Atlanta next month spending Thanksgiving with us, along with my 2 "sista-cousins" (one of which is cool, the other I could live without, sorry), including my mom. Lord, that's a lot of people. I'm not quite sure if I'm ready to serve and entertain family. But, everyone else is so gung ho about the idea — my husband, son, the sista-cousins who I haven't seen in forever. Even my Mama's cool, but asking me if I'm ready for guests. I don't want to be the oddball out, again — the unthankful grinch who stole Thanksgiving. I'll figure out how to get ready...

This will be my first time in the same room with "family" now that I've begun my healing and surrendered my mask. Jesus... what a scary thought, I gave up my mask smh.

I'm really nervous about this and have already had to fight off two panic attacks this week just thinking about it — being at the table with folks, fake smiling as I *pass the greens* — and we're a good month away! Ugh, it just does something to my spirit. So, if you could please pray for my mental state, I'd appreciate it.

Man... what just happened to my life, again? Everything was going fairly smooth, ya girl had a nice rhythm and balance... then BAM!

It's this healing business...

God's got jokes.
This one ain't cute or funny.

M

Chapter 53

On Thu, Nov 2, 2006 at 4:35 PM Krystal Ashe wrote:

Hey Mikki,

Ok, sis. We can put off the meetup. No worries at all, but this is interesting, sis...

You seemed genuinely excited about our in-person meet up before — girl, I was ready to get in some good shopping and good food with great company!

So, hmmph. I don't know exactly what happened, but I'm sensing that whatever went down in session with Jamilah, you're experiencing some fierce resistance right now.

The tone of your email feels like you've received some *truth* or *instruction* that's challenging you beyond where you are and what's familiar to you. Now, fear is settling in your heart.

Don't let it, Mikki! Be encouraged and ask yourself these key questions:

- Has Jamilah ever done anything or led you in a direction that hurt you?
- Do you still believe that she has your best healing interest at heart?
- Could you have gotten this far without her being your guide?

On the spiritual tip, let's be real, sis. The enemy is not afraid of our progress here and there. As long as we keep taking 5 steps back for every 2 steps forward, he's cool with that. Cycles of joy work for him —as long as we eventually return to brokenness and depression.

Now. What *really* bothers the devil is the thought of a FREE, HEALED, AND WHOLE YOU that escapes his grasps for good and can now free others with your testimony. "Free women" are a problem to him, sis!

I know that, while we're in it, the last thing we're thinking about is helping someone else when there are days we feel like *we're* drowning. We can barely breathe some days on the journey to the finish line. But, we must be mindful that the enemy never just looks at you. He's playing a numbers game, sis. His strategy is — "for every 1 person I can keep bound by childhood trauma and sexual abuse, I can keep ## more people from ever getting close to realizing their freedom."

Remember what I told you in February, Mikki... surrender to the healing process. It's the only way to reach that finish line. Trust the process, you're still in good hands with God.

Praying for you,
Krystal

Chapter 54

On Sun, Nov 5, 2006 at 6:27 AM Mikki Jones wrote:

Thanks, Krystal.

I appreciate you. Always will...

M

Chapter 55

On Fri, Nov 10, 2006 at 11:16 PM Mikki Jones wrote:

Krystal!

Am I wrong?

You know the sista-cousin I told you about, Tammy? We just don't gel well together.

For one, Tammy runs her mouth too much (gets it from her mother). Now, her sister, Rae? Raevyn was my girl growing up. When I would spend the weekend over, my uncle used to call us all inside with just two names, "Mikki & TammyRae!" We knew that meant for everybody to come inside and wash up for dinner, and all the other kids had to go home. You would think they were twins, but they are oh so different.

So, Tammy reached out today and asked to crash at my house — girl, I told her absolutely not! That's what my insides were screaming (actually my insides said, hell to the nahhh!), but I managed to decline nicely. The nerve. She knows we don't even get along like that.

It's not about us having the room. It wasn't about her giving us enough notice to make preparations. It's not about her wanting to "*catch up with my nephew who's so big now.*" Girl bye. And, I can't invite Rae without inviting Tammy, could I? Naww, my uncle and his nosey wife would call me out and start asking a bunch of questions. Rae already knows how I feel about her messy sister. I just wish Rae and I could hang without her older sister tagging along like a hall monitor, and hogging all the conversations like she knows everything. Just like old times smh...

I should be able to control the atmosphere in my doggone house and keep people away who disturb my spirit. Right? Shhhoooot. I'm the Queen of this here castle! I run this!

Jamilah called it this week. She said in that soft, motherly voice, "*Mikki, you're entering a season of one of the biggest hurdles on your healing journey — family. Pace yourself, brace yourself for impact in very sensitive places that are still on the mend and haven't been tested. You may experience some friction, agitation, you may even want to lash out. Breathe through it and remember. You are safe. You are loved. You are supported...*"

Mannn, she wasn't lying. This family visit is something I really can't put into words for many reasons. If I can just wake up in my right mind on Black Friday and this is all over, it will be a miracle.

Keep praying for me, sis!

I'm sorry, I didn't even ask how you're doing, how your holiday plans are coming along. Lordy. Do you have big plans for the holidays, Krystal?

CHAPTER 55

Mikki

Chapter 56

On Thu, Nov 16, 2006 at 9:33 AM Krystal Ashe wrote:

Mikki,

You're doing great, girl! You're facing this hurdle, however high it is for you, and you're doing so with much more assurance and confidence than you would have handled things in, say, January, February. Right?

So, go ahead and pat yourself on the back, sis; look at the progress you've made and are still making! Weren't you the one locked up in your room, depressed and suicidal, doubtful that you'd ever make it past that point? Now, look at you! Entertaining family? Now you're the hostess with the most-est? I am sooo proud of you, girl!

And, yes ma'am! You *are* the Queen of your castle and you have every right and full authority to protect the peace of your safe place as much as you like. Your cousin Tammy will adjust, she'll be okay. And, cool cousin Rae? She will understand as well. We're all adults, here.

Keep the main thing the main thing — get through Thanksgiving Day with your sanity. Your family loves you, all of them in their own special way. See if you can find a place of gratitude for family in your heart, however difficult that may be. Just try, you've got this!

While I'll be praying for you, please return the favor, sis! I seem to have my own special *family* dynamics to deal with...

Quiet as it's kept, I've been separated from my husband for some time now, about 10 months — different residences, limited contact. Recently, we reconnected, and surprisingly, the conversation has been like talking to a different person, a man I don't know, in a good way, feel me? Go figure.

Don't worry, I'm not getting all excited. I remember from whence I've come, and I have too much going on right now to go back there. It's just dinner. Nothing more, nothing less. I'm happy for him and the work he's been doing. So, yeah. There's that.

Keep me posted, Mikki. Girl, don't email me next week talking 'bout you turned Thanksgiving out! No ma'am LOL! The finish line is just ahead. That alone is something to be thankful for.

Krystal

Chapter 57

On Wed, Nov 22, 2006 at 10:48 PM Mikki Jones wrote:

Well, Krystal.

Hey.

I've done all the praying I can do. I've stared in the mirror for hours and said all the scriptures and affirmations I could think of. I've asked for God's grace and mercy. I thought about reaching out to Jamilah a couple of times; I think that sista's on vacation in the islands somewhere doing a detox. Who can blame her, she needs a good Caribbean exhale.

Sooo. It's all going down tomorrow. My greens are slow cooking, and the turkey is stuffed and seasoned to perfection. The house is clean, especially my baseboards (you know how your Mama always judges how clean your house is by the baseboards LOL). I probably shouldn't be up too too late, I'll need my strength. The busyness of cooking and getting the house prepared for my uncle and family is a welcomed distraction keeping my mind off things...

Krystal, you ever wish you could jump in your car, back out the driveway, hit the road to anywhere, and never look back? That's how a part of me feels right now. I feel like running away. My grown behind self wants to jump in the car and skiiiiid off to the interstate and just riiiiiide. Funny. That's probably that same part of me that thought this healing process would kill me. It hasn't so far, and now after getting some needed help, I have a bigger, stronger part of me to talk that small, fragile part down... 'cause she's a trip.

Anyway, I'm just taking a quick break to say hi. I appreciate all of your prayers and words of encouragement, Krystal. They have helped tremendously. Not many can find a friend like you, someone who lets you borrow their strength when you have none left. For that, I am very grateful for you being in my life right now. God connected me with just what I needed, and for that...

Thank you, Lord.

P.S. Blessings to you and yours. Hope all goes well with... dinner :).

Chapter 58

On Fri, Nov 24, 2006 at 10:41 AM Krystal Ashe wrote:

Happy Black Friday, sis!

Honey, you made it! How did you survive Thanksgiving? I started to reach out last night before bed, but I figured you were probably worn out and ecstatic all at the same time. You made it through the day, yes? God is good!

I was shonuff praying for you, sis. How'd it go?

K

Chapter 59

On Sat, Nov 25, 2006 at 9:19 PM Krystal Ashe wrote:

Hey, Mikki!

You there? Still recuperating? Is everything OK?

K

Chapter 60

On Wed, Nov 29, 2006 at 11:50 PM Mikki Jones wrote:

I'm so sorry, Krystal. I need more time. I'm ok.

I'll be in touch before the weekend...

M

Chapter 61

On Sat, Dec 2, 2006 at 1:03 AM Mikki Jones wrote:

I don't know how to say this to you, Krystal. I told Jamilah everything yesterday in session. She said just come clean and own it. So, here goes nothing...

I lied.

I wasn't 100% with you, myself about Thanksgiving, and for that, I want to apologize.

I know it's a waste of time to spend almost a year now emailing *me* back and forth, especially if I'm not gonna be honest. I remember our conversation about masks in May, and how you prayed that God would continue to *crack my mask and heal me.* Right now? I have felt the weight of that prayer all week, crushing every desperate attempt to keep hiding from the truth and burying secret after secret.

If you will allow me to come clean, I will.

So. I told you that my uncle, his wife, and my cousins, Tammy and Rae were coming over to the house for Thanksgiving. And they did. That was the truth. But, it wasn't the whole truth. It wasn't "my uncle, the father figure".

I think one of the hardest things to do for anyone who's been molested by a family member is to come clean while that family member and/or others are still alive. It's like you're already feeling weird about what happened, right? You're feening for a crystal ball to show you how things would go if you 'tell it', and you're trying really hard to hold on to any semblance of family connection and acceptance you still have. All in the only brain you have.

You begin to fear backlash, being ostracized, being the "cause" of hurting so many people you care about. You feel that some kinfolk will look at you like, "*It happened when? You're how old now? Chile, you might as well had taken that to your grave! Why now?!*"

And you know the usual suspects — it's all those gossipy aunts, them nosey cousins like Tammy, and that jealous sibling needs to hear to start some mess with you. So, you don't really want to come clean because everyone will be pissed at you at best — or they'll outright hate you at worse. And these are the very people you want to love you.

I am so sorry. My little diversion a few emails back about my "uncle" was my natural coping mechanism to a painful truth. I thought I was strong enough now to speak the truth. But, the intention of speaking the truth was quickly shut down by shame and the fear of backlash for making the family look bad.

Like I said, I told Jamilah what I'd done. I'm working through this now, and just the fact that I'm coming clean to you is progress.

166

Needless to say, Jamilah gave me a good talking to yesterday. In addition to her, "The sooner the better" speech about you , she ended the session with:

> *"No one can speak truth to what you have felt or experienced like you can, Mikki. And until you do, that little girl will always be imprisoned inside of you. So, instead of being her tough warden, locking her behind your masks and stories, it's time for you to be her warrior. Be her hero, Mikki..."*

So, that little girl in the 4th-grade with long pigtails and big glasses — it's time to rescue her from me and remind her how valuable God knows she is.

I'm sorry for lying to you, making up stories about my family. Here's the truth, Krystal.

My "uncle" is not my uncle or my father-figure. He's my biological father — yes, he's still alive. A part of my father died to me, or maybe a part of me died to him when he got married when I was in my teens, so it was easier on my mind to describe him to people as my "uncle" — especially if they'd never meet him in person. Next session, I begin the work of reclaiming the time I lost when I felt abandoned and betrayed by my father at 15.

Because the bottom line is this... Nothing tells a little girl you're hopelessly worthless, you will <u>never</u> be believed, and you're now a second-class daughter quite like when your father marries your molester.

M

Chapter 62

On Sat, Dec 2, 2006 at 7:16 AM Krystal Ashe wrote:

Lord, Mikki. Good morning, sis.

I keep reading your email over and over. Maybe I need coffee. I'm trying to make sense of it all, meanwhile, my stomach keeps balling up into a tight knot at what I think you're saying.

I'm at a complete loss for words right now, but I think I understand what you're trying to tell me. And please correct me if I've got it wrong, Mikki...

Are you saying... you found the strength to be a gracious host, serving Thanksgiving dinner in your home with a smile like everything's peachy — to your actual father (not your uncle) and his wife and their kids, and his wife is the family member who molested you as a child? The one we first talked about back in January?

K

Chapter 63

On Sat, Dec 2, 2006 at 12:03 PM Mikki Jones wrote:

Yep. That one, Krystal. The one who changed the entire course of my childhood innocence.

They all left and returned to Cali last Saturday. I thought the return of some distance would help me breathe a little easier. But, there are still moments where it feels like I'm boiling in anger. The top of my head and the bottom of my feet are red hot. Because it wasn't just about what she did *to* me, it was also about introduction and exposure.

See, as a child, when you're spoon-fed pornography like Gerber's applesauce, and you've licked the spoon clean, that ~~shit~~, sorry, crap infects your system. Sure, as most 9-year-olds would do, it all begins with finger-pointing, giggles, and a lot of "Ewww, that's nasty!" But, when a lustful, erotic seed is planted in children, it grows like poisonous wildflowers. Curiosity breeds a thirst your eyes can't quench, and you never know the damage till later and the tears you'll cry because your innocence has been ravaged by it. I wanted it. It kept calling me.

And now, here I was at Thanksgiving 2006 with my pusher. Just surreal.

Sitting across the table from each other, talking, eating, laughing —*like it never happened*. But, it did.

In the back of my mind, no lie, Krystal, I kept asking myself, "*Does this heffa even remember what happened? Did she have a nervous stomach with the bubble guts at just the thought of being in* **my** *presence, coming into* **my** *house, to look* **me** *in the eyes, to sit and eat at* **my** *table? At any point during the day, was she going to pull me to the side privately and say, 'you know, what happened when you were a kid was f^*&!@ up, and I'm sorry'*"?

Nope. And maybe that's what made me even angrier on the inside... that she was so nice, so calm... so normal. I was legit offended. Like, how could she be here and not sweat bullets? I mean, she was respectful to me as the lady of the house, but a part of me wanted to see her squirm. Just being honest.

I know you won't judge me harshly, Krystal, but the thought did run through my head a couple of times... Maybe, at the height of conversation and laughter, I would clank the fork against my glass, and at a quiet table with all eyes on me, I'd expose her nice, pleasant self and tell everyone what she did to me.

Then... you ready? I'd dramatically scoot my chair back from the table, sashay out the front door like a pregnant prostitute clown LOL, and skiiid away in my car like I wanted to do on Thanksgiving Eve.

BAM! Mic dropped !

It didn't exactly go that way, though.

I blame God, He blocked all of my shenanigans. All those scriptures I meditated on and spoke out loud in front of the mirror the night before

—messed up my sinister plans. Without God, I would have turned Thanksgiving out! Would you have done the same thing?

Between God in one ear, and Jamilah in the other, I can see the finish line coming closer. I'm really trying to grow, sis, and it's good to be talking with God again. The closer I get to Him, the farther I'll get from my past and every crutch holding me back. Like Jamilah says, "The sooner the better."

I'm still human and going through a gumbo of emotions after that ordeal. But somehow, with God's help and the best scraped-together fake smile I could find, I lived.

Mikki

Chapter 64

On Sun, Dec 3, 2006 at 6:36 PM Krystal Ashe wrote:

Good for you, Mikki. That took a lot for you to come all the way clean — with yourself.

You're not the first person who's had to go through this, and you won't be the last.

If it's any consolation... girl, Jamilah had to chin-check my stories on many occasions. Whenever I'd dodge the truth, she'd say, "*Ohhh my beloved black women! You are some of the most creative people on the planet!*"

It's true, LOL! We either create greatness or bring chaos to life. We know how to craft a narrative (read: lie) that not only makes us feel good but it protects our sanity until we can do better. It's crazy how we learn this tactic so young. It's all a part of our healing process.

Learning how to truthfully verbalize what happened, or in your case, I can fully imagine you trying to type your email and tell what happened in its truest form — stopping, starting, backspacing, and re-typing your words. Listen, I completely get it. No apologies needed.

I remember when Jamilah put me on the Forgiveness Diet and I was in the process of writing these words for the first time, "*I forgive you, white boys, for snatching me in those bushes at knifepoint.*" My fingers started to cramp up and I got nauseated. With tears running down my face, I put the pen down and started stretching my fingers out and balling up my fist, real fast.

I looked down at that un-finished line, "*I forgive you white boys...*", and began to pound that white sheet of notebook paper with my fists. Sis, I just couldn't write what they did. Doing so felt like I had slung myself back there in the bushes all over again. Only this time, I wanted to hurt them. Beat them. Stab them with their own knife.

But, all I had in front of me was a stupid sheet of white notebook paper. See, Mikki? We eventually get to the bottom of the truth, just like I found a way to finish that line. You initially did what was safe for you, calling your father your 'uncle' to a person who would never know the difference. Girl, you were only protecting your mental health and your injured place at that moment.

What I am so proud to see is your ability and strength to do a few things, like:

1. Re-evaluate whether the status quo of secrets and stories still serves you.
2. Re-assess the value of acting out in anger and rage versus the choice of self-control.
3. Renegotiate how much freedom you actually deserve.

To stay committed to healing trauma after a face-off with your offender, you had to question yourself... *Am I finally sick and tired of being sick and tired? Have I grown weary of always fronting? Can I develop such disdain for my lies that they make me throw up in my mouth? Why should I stay in the prison this situation built, while everyone else walks?*

And, you answered every question like the beautiful, worthy, evolving woman you are.

Don't stop now... let's keep going!

Krystal

Chapter 65

On Mon, Dec 11, 2006 at 10:56 PM Mikki Jones wrote:

Hey Krystal,

So, I had another fight with God yesterday... at church no less, lordy. This renewed relationship with God is going to be a piece of cake... said no one, ever LOL!

Some of the worst distractions happen at church. You're trying to get into the praise and worship or the sermon, and your mind is racing. You've got questions. You've got... things on your heart that you don't understand. That's why I wanted to be there amongst the body of Christ.

The preacher was reading from Psalm 23 and had gotten down to verse 5, describing the decadent table that God has prepared for us in the presence of our enemies.

I don't know where this thought came from, but my spirit whispered to God, "*You had me prepare a table before <u>You</u> — in the presence of my worst enemy...*"

The preacher was going on about the abundant varieties of comforts at the table and all of the rich blessings for our choosing... while I was rolling my eyes, getting madder and madder about serving *her* my good greens and turkey and macaroni and cheese and...

Before I knew it, God interrupted my train of thought with the strangest question.

How was I going to answer *this*? It kinda felt like how you described your forgiveness ceremony. For me, the entire church shifted, and it was just me and God in the room. I felt summoned to Divine Court to take the witness stand and answer this enigma:

"What do you do when your worst enemy becomes My friend, Mikki?

...I sat there gut-punched, looking dumb. No air to speak. I just kept silent.

"What do you do when you call them 'my molester', and I call them, 'My beloved.'?
Whose ownership wins... yours or Mine?"

It was then I was able to put together why I was so mad at her nice, calm demeanor during Thanksgiving. She was God's property now. She had accepted Jesus Christ as Lord and Savior — and God never got permission from *me* to forgive her! Out of all my years of suffering, God never consulted me, never asked me if I thought she was worthy to be forgiven and released from *my* prison.

By this time, I'm weeping almost uncontrollably.

He took my hand to help me step down from the witness stand. I was led into a room filled with TV screens. On them, I could see vignettes of my worse moments — all of the times where I failed, where I let God down, where I did some nasty, dishonest, crazy embarrassing things that no one knows about but God. He continued...

"Even if others knew your sins, the way you know about My beloved's sins, they couldn't stop My gift of grace and mercy for you! Because I love you just that much and My love covers all!"

Sis, by the time I came back to myself, I was at the altar for prayer. The ushers must've seen me doubled-over in tears, and escorted me to the front with the crowd.

God: A trillion
Mikki: Zero

Gratefully, I lost the fight, sis, and I learned some hard truths in the process yesterday, for instance:

- Prideful anger is poison in the heart of the one who carries and nurtures it —even legitimate victims of trauma and sexual abuse.
- God's end game is not to justify our right to hurt, or validate our thirst for revenge, but to establish His power to heal.
- Pride will always have you looking foolish, thinking you're big and bad enough to enter the ring against God. I am not in God's weight class (read: "girl, go sit down before you're sat down LOL!")
- God is grown! He is God all by Himself —without my help, permission, or approval.

I can't help but wonder... Could this be why I was so sick with depression, suicidal thoughts, low self-esteem...? I had eaten the rotten fruit of pride and swallowed the seeds whole. Then, sick as a dog, I thought I could spar with God? Not smart.

Whew! Girl, I finally see what you meant when you said you heard your *judge's robe rip* back in March. Now God's Kingdom can come since we've both been dethroned; we've been knocked off our imaginary pedestals back to our proper place.

Guess what, sis? I think I'm ready to dive into your 2nd book, *Renouncing Victimhood.* Being a victim no longer serves me.

I repent and turn away from that mindset, Lord.

M

Chapter 66

On Fri, Dec 15, 2006 at 4:10 PM Krystal Ashe wrote:

Hey sis!

Yeah, unfortunately, *Renouncing Victimhood* is not a book you can read from the comfort of your *own throne* LOL!

But, girl, once you lay down your crown and have reached the point where you're ready to surrender to healing, look out! The book guides you on how to assume and maintain the proper position, while the Great Physician removes the tumors of trauma.

It's like a mother giving birth while sitting straight up in a chair, or someone having heart surgery while lying on their stomach... it just won't work, and that's what we've done! We've obstructed the healing we so desperately want and need —kicking, squirming, and acting out of our pain. If we'd simply surrender to the process, the IV with all the healing goodness we need can be administered to our soul.

Once we're able to just lie there and trust that God knows what He's doing, that's when real *healing happens* (as Jamilah would say LOL).

Never forget how far you've come in a year, Mikki. From depression, suicide planning — girl, you already had your husband's new wife picked out, remember that? You tried to back out of this process so many times, but you found a way to hang in there and trust the process towards your finish line.

You're ready. Now you can stop roaming around in an open cage.

You, sis, are free to go! Now, rise from the ashes... spread your own wings, and learn how to soar!

Krystal

Chapter 67

On Wed, Dec 27, 2006 at 10:42 PM Mikki Jones wrote:

"Beloved, you do know that many people pitch a tent at the finish line, in pursuit of... the finish line?"

Krystal, tonight's session was all about the *finish line*. At first, I wondered if Jamilah was talking about me, pitching a tent. Yeah, she was. You and I have talked and talked (or typed) about *the finish line* since February.

Back then, I thought the finish line was this invisible, unreachable line drawn in the sand dividing two worlds: one, the end of the dark world of clinical depression and suicide, and two, the beginning of the bright and beautiful world of being trauma-free.

Apparently, this line of thinking missed an important vantage point.

"Ok, Mikki. That's good. But, have you considered that the finish line is not just about endings, but about perspectives."

Interesting. Jamilah was right, sis. My pitched tent and I were already *at* the end —the end of hope, the end of trying, the end of wanting to live. But, I wasn't *finished* yet!

It's weird, but... Jamilah helped me to see that the finish line was under my control all along. It was a line drawn by me and my decisions alone. Once I was finished fighting God on the operating table, as you say, once I was finished trying to punish others for my pain, once I was finished honoring the pain as the only real, dependable constant I knew, that's the *finish line* where *healing happens.*

So, that was my first "light bulb" perspective on my finish line tonight. Then...

Jamilah handed me a piece of paper and a blue ink pen, and said, *"Before we cross over into a new perspective of your journey, is there anything else you need to say to anyone? Think forgiveness diet. I'll give you a few moments alone."*

Jamilah walked out the room and left me in the care of the Lady in Blue on her wall, still kneeling in aqua-blue water, both hands lifted toward a cloudless blue sky and a big, yellow sun-circle above her head.

I kept thinking... *"Is there anything else I need to say to anyone?*

What came to mind was... our conversation on 12/2 and the Thanksgiving ordeal. That's when I realized that I, too, had an *un-finished line* that needed my attention.

I scribbled it on the paper and waited for Jamilah to return. I looked up at the Lady in Blue, proud. I could see a reflection of my surrender in hers.

After thousands of lines of forgiveness, on pages and pages of notebook paper, for seven days and seven nights, I had finally reached this particular *finish line*. It was time to resurrect my father, raise him up permanently from the demoted position of "uncle", to his rightful place as a forgiven father.

> "I forgive you, Dad, totally and unconditionally for not knowing what you could never know when you married her."

See, sometimes the *finish* line is not a line drawn in the sand at all. The *line* is words, phrases, maybe a complete sentence you need to say that marks the completion of the matter, so you can move on. There. I said it.

"So, Krystal's un-finished line was 'I forgive you white boys...' Right? Are you sure this is your un-finished line?"

It was. And we had the final forgiveness ceremony with my now *finished* line. I spoke the words aloud from the paper; Jamilah (as my dad) affirmed me, apologized for what was not known, and asked for my forgiveness.

She then told me not to worry about my relationship with my dad any longer — *"Love will save the day and heal the years. God is love."*

Before I left, Jamilah laid out what seemed like her biggest ask of my journey, all in that sweet, calm voice. Preparation for what's next in my life... and apparently, some things and some people I have to leave behind in order to move forward. They just can't go with me.

"*Now, beloved. Go home. Stop sending those emails back and forth. Rebuild with your husband, family, and friends. It's time for you to reconnect with the real world and real people who love you and support you. You know what you have to do—the sooner the better.*"

M

Chapter 68

On Sat, Dec 30, 2006 at 8:11 PM Mikki Jones wrote:

This is weird. I guess it always was, right?
But no, no I won't judge it. This is what I needed in order to cope.

Now. How do you say good-bye, let go, break up... with a piece of yourself?

I wanted to say something back on 10/27, when I knew this day was coming; when I knew clearly that I'd have to let *us* go. See, it's what Jamilah meant by "the sooner the better." For her, the thought of "Mikki and Krystal" doing a face-to-face meetup would have been the opportune time for me to face *myself* and walk away clean, in my own *Mikki* strength.

But, the thought of letting the emails go right around the time of Thanksgiving was too much for me. I desperately needed to borrow *someone's* strength to help me get over that hump. Who else could I trust at such a monumental moment? Could I trust a stronger, healed *version* of me?

Wow. Almost one year of conversations where I could be totally butt-naked, vulnerable, and find relief from the pain —within another part of myself. The strong *character* I always imagined having. Eventually, I stopped worrying about the hidden email hackers, just give me my Gmail account and the persona of Krystal Ashe!

Speaking of those unseen, ghost readers I so feared would learn my truth LOL — now I need them to learn the truth and sever the stronghold of secrets that may be wrapped around *their* wings!... Eavesdrop on that LOL!

Do I walk away from convos with Krystal 100% healed? Nahh. I have at least 3-6 more months to go with Jamilah, maybe more. She believes it's time for me to walk these last few miles on my own, in my own strength. Pretty scary. I haven't done that in a year, not in a real sense.

So, nope, the work ain't over. I don't think it ever will be. I may not be 100% healed yet, but I am 100% convinced that the **maintenance** required for Trauma Overcomers is ongoing. I feel like I'm moving ahead to a life of victory to victory —because there will always be an enemy who tries to un-bury your pain in order to bury your purpose. And my escort to victory? It will always be God's glory.

Me and God are growing closer. I will never forget during my "curse God and die" phase, how God drew nearer to me. How cool is that? He didn't run away, and He didn't throw me away. That prayer on 1/14, "Let's help her, please", God the Father, Son, Holy Spirit, and a host of angels came to my rescue! And, they didn't wait until I got my life right, or got my mouth right... God was close to my broken spirit. He showed up to bottle every tear to water a future harvest that will blow my mind. I could put a praise right there!

And so it is. It's time to say thank you and good-bye. I'm excited to make new memories. No more consulting the past about my future. I've received all that this season of writing emails back and forth to myself had to offer. Now I enter a beautiful place where I have the power to create real beauty and freedom for my life.

I trust that if God has promised to transform me from glory to glory, then every *glory* has a finish line. That finish line leads to the *once upon a time* that begins the next glorious journey. Funny how the story of glory works... it's always to be continued.

Good-bye, Krystal Ashe.

Hello. I am Mikki Jones.

VIII

Begin Again

Get ready. Set. Begin. Again.
As usual, without rewind.
Without borrowed strength.
In the full embodiment of YOU.

Chapter 69

November 12, 2010

Dear Jamilah Jordan and Mikki Jones:

The National Sexual Abuse Research Association (NSARA) is pleased to announce that your abstract entitled, *Like it Never Happened: Strength in Story-Telling and Fictional Characters for Abuse Survivors,* has been accepted for both publication and presentation at next year's NSARA 2011 National Conference in Washington, D.C. on February 16–18, 2011.

Your research on the divided consciousness of abuse victims between hope and despair, and how trauma story-telling as the healed version of themselves offers a viable pathway to healing is both noteworthy and beneficial to the mental health community.

Assistance with travel arrangements is available by contacting travel@nsara.org. The specific details of the day and time of your presentation will be included in the conference program which will be available in January. All accepted publications will be included in the Conference Proceeding Booklet with ISBN number.

Thank you for your interest in participating in NSARA 2011, and we look forward to seeing you in Washington, D.C. next year.

Sincere regards,

Dr. Landon Best, Executive Director
The National Sexual Abuse Research Association (NSARA)
lbest@nsara.org
202-55-NSARA (202-556-7272)

IX

Drafts Folder

Drafts

This is crazy.... What am I doing right now? Like, who could I send this to for help?

What would it be like to be healed, whole, free — to be normal without traumatic childhood memories always creeping up on me. What would *that* Mikki sound like? What would she feel like? Could she help me?

I've been thinking about *her* for days now. I wish I could talk to her.

I wish she could guide me to that elusive, faraway land called Freedom. I wish she could show me how to make it outta this mess and tell me that everything is going to be alright. Because *that Mikki* knows me. She would know the possibilities my mind can't seem to grasp right now. She holds the keys to overcoming trauma — the ones that I can only hear jingling in the distance.

Maybe I could divvy up some of my madness. Let's see. I'd give her age 5, and I'll keep age 9. Yeah. I'd borrow her strength to babysit the white boys for me while I deal with family. Is that even an even exchange,

Mikki? I dunno. But trying to handle the damage of these two events, at the same time, is driving me crazy!

She would be crystal clear, though, on how to handle my childhood experiences without doing further damage to my spirit. Oh, how my spirit longs to rise from these ashes, the pain of being re-burned over and over again. If I don't heal, and soon, this shit right here is gonna take me out forever.

Who on earth could I trust to be *crystal* clear — no tryouts and wanna be's — on how to support me, guide me, help me rise from the *ashes* of trauma?

Drafts

This is crazy.... What am I doing right now? Like, who could I send this to for help?

What would it be like to be healed, whole, free — to be normal without traumatic childhood memories always creeping up on me. What would *that* Mikki sound like? What would she feel like? Could she help me?

I've been thinking about her for days now. I wish I could talk to her.

I wish she could guide me to that elusive, faraway land called Freedom. I wish she could show me how to make it outta this mess and tell me that everything is going to be alright. Because *that Mikki* knows me. She would know the possibilities my mind can't seem to grasp right now. She holds the keys to overcoming trauma — the ones that I can only hear jingling in the distance.

Maybe I could divvy up some of my madness. Let's see. I'd give her age 5, and I'll keep age 9. Yeah. I'd borrow her strength to babysit the white boys for me while I deal with family. Is that even an even exchange,

Mikki? I dunno. But trying to handle the damage of these two events, at the same time, is driving me crazy!

She would be crystal clear, though, on how to handle my childhood experiences without doing further damage to my spirit. Oh, how my spirit longs to rise from these ashes, the pain of being re-burned over and over again. If I don't heal, and soon, this shit right here is gonna take me out forever.

Who on earth could I trust to be *crystal* clear — no tryouts and wanna be's — on how to support me, guide me, help me rise from the *ashes* of trauma? Maybe she's an acclaimed author on childhood trauma and sexual abuse? A highly sought-after speaker and lecturer who inspires people around the world?

Krystal Ashe? Krystal with a K? Yeah. She could borrow a k from the center of Mikki lol.

Funny.

This just might work...

Drafts

Draft saved Wed, Jan 11, 2006 at 11:11 AM

Dear Ms. Ashe:

Hi. You don't know me, but I really need your help.

Afterword: The Soundtrack

I pray this book has touched you, especially readers who have experienced childhood trauma and sexual abuse.

Perhaps *Someone Borrowed, Someone Blue* touched you in a place you didn't want to acknowledge existed; I know the feeling. Or, maybe a place you didn't want to be disturbed — but it desperately needed to be shaken up, and now you realize that *healing happens.*

Selah! You will reach *your* finish line, too. Borrow my victory over trauma and childhood sexual abuse that you've just read about in these pages of fiction. Lean into Mikki and Krystal's points of view, knowing you're not crazy or alone. Glean nuggets here and there from Jamilah, and *take Jesus with you to counseling.*

Yes, I invite you to do all of that. But, if you want an even closer, more transparent glimpse into my healing process, listen to *Someone Borrowed, Someone Blue: The Soundtrack.*

In true "Mikki" fashion (Mikki — "Kim" backward minus an 'm'), I threw everything I had at the pain, including creativity. There's nothing like living in a double-mind where on one side, you're planning your suicide, and on the other, you're creating music to help you... live.

The soundtrack for this book is just that. These songs were written, produced, and performed by me between 2006 — 2009, at the height of the clinical depression, suicidal thoughts, "Thanksgiving dinners", and therapy. That tiny, strong place in me was determined to use every creative drop I had to heal, and thus, these songs were born.

When you listen to *"Mikki's Prayer"* (see *Chapters 42-43*), you hear the only syllable lyrics I could muster — telling God what happened in those bushes, praying that He'd save me before I go under for good. He did. Now, this prayer song belongs to all who want to speak to God about their trauma, but can't find the words.

Listen closely. Hear the ticking clock in *"Thinkin' of You"* (see *Drafts Folder*)? I dreamed this song one night — thinking of a healed, whole me — like Krystal. And yet, it's also a song about how God spends His days having innumerable thoughts about us (Psalm 139:17-18).

Finally, hear the victory and gratitude in *"A Beautiful Place"* (*Chapter 68*) — that place previously smothered by secrets and masks that now celebrates the power to create *real* beauty and freedom.

So, if you ever hear a key ring jingling off in the distance, while you feel trapped behind the bars of your circumstances, listen intently. It's either one of two things — or both.

That's the sound of the gifts that God has given you to soothe your soul and find strength in those tough moments. Or, it's the testimony of others who were exactly where you are and made it to freedom.

Headphones on! I'm grateful to share the *sound of my keys* with you. It's your turn to use them....

Love,
KB

Scan to listen

Made in the USA
Columbia, SC
31 May 2021